I0676824

Murder at Mother's

Maighread MacKay

0

Cover Designer: GetCovers.com

Contact the Author:

Website: https://www.mhefferman.ca

FB: www.facebook.com/maighreadmackay

Twitter: @maighreadmackay

Linkedin: https://www.linkedin.com/in/margaret-hefferman-65003b29/

Murder at Mother's:
ISBN: 9780973979268

Dear Readers,

Some of my fondest memories are the times my mother read to me before going to bed. When I was little, she would read Maggie Muggins or the Bobbsey Twins books. Being of an inquisitive mind, I relished the mystery of the stories. As I grew, the Nancy Drew and Hardy Boys books attracted my attention. One of my favourites, **Nancy Drew, and the Ghost of Blackwood Hall,** brought me a love of ghost stories and the unexplained which has continued to this day. My current novel, **Murder at Mother's,** introduces a ghost: a feisty woman who is not about to take her murder lying down! She and her unearthly sidekick, Gladys, do all they can to solve the murder before moving on to the light. This book wouldn't have seen the light of day without the valuable expertise of the following:

First and foremost, my fabulous editor, **Sue Reynolds** who understands what I'm trying to share in my books and encourages me with her positive feedback and assistance with revision.

DC Murray Marling (ret.), a dear friend who helped me with police procedures. If there are mistakes, they are totally mine.

The Durham Regional Police, Central Division, and the Emergency Services for Durham Region. (Oh, the things one must ask when they're the author of a murder mystery.)

The Institute of Forensic Sciences, Toronto, and **Dr. Anita Lal** for her valuable forensic insight, especially when talking about poisons.

Durham Farm Connections for their farming and veterinarian advice.

Precision Auto, Brooklin, for answering my questions about brakes and brake linings.

The ranch described is loosely based on an actual horse and dog sanctuary in King City, Ontario which is called **Dog Tales**. The description of the festival in May is from their own festival held each August. To read more about this wonderful place, please go to http://www.dogtales.ca/.

I thoroughly enjoyed writing this book and meeting my characters. I hope that you will enjoy it as well and perhaps think a bit about what might happen on the other side.

Yours 'til next time,

Maighread

Dedication

This book is dedicated to my husband, Graydon.
With encouragement and affection, he has been my best friend
and companion for over 50 years.
I'm so glad we shared this journey together.

Be kind, for everyone you meet
is fighting a hard battle.
- Philo

A simple act of caring creates an endless ripple - Anonymous.

Kindness is a language.
which the deaf can hear and the blind can see.
— Mark Twain

He descended into Hell.
– The Apostle's Creed

Chapter One

The fire was the first incident that caught Martha's attention. One of the ranch hands needed a rope from the tack room and arrived in time to smell smoke and dampen the blaze. A few weeks later, Jared discovered a fence bordering the back forty was down. He repaired it before any of the horses escaped. She shivered as she thought about the danger they'd be in wandering around the forest at night. Both episodes could have been accidents.

Today, dressed in her favourite jeans and boots, Martha strode down the hill to the horses. As she walked, her cane stirred the dry ground with small circular puffs of sand. Her heart and pace were more accelerated than usual as she thought about her beloved mare.

Her first baby. Wonder how she'll take to being a mother? Jared said the delivery went well, but I'll feel better once I've seen Gracie for myself.

As she approached the barn door, she heard a call. "Grandma, look out!" Forceful hands grabbed her in a firm grip. Her cane went flying. Her hair lifted as something whizzed past her ear and caused a burning sensation where it grazed her arm. She clutched the arms which held her and looked up into the shocked eyes of her grandson.

"What happened?"

"A truck tire was bouncing down the hill and heading straight for you. A few more seconds and you'd be laying on the ground."

"A truck tire?"

"Yes."

"Where on earth did it come from?"

"Don't know. Let me look at you." Jared set his grandmother back from him and examined her. "Your shirt's torn and you've got a nasty scrape on your arm. Charli's in back with Gracie and the colt. C'mon –

0

let's get you cleaned up and then I'll look around to see where the tire came from."

Jared picked up the cane and gave it to Martha. Still shaking from the encounter, she took his arm as they walked the length of the stable to the stall which housed the mare and foal. Charli looked up from brushing the horse.

"Grandma, what's wrong? Your shirt's torn and you're shaking."

Martha plunked down onto a bale of hay, laying her cane beside her, while she explained what had happened.

Jared said, "Could you look after Grandma, Charli? I'm going to see what I can find out."

"Sure. Let me get the first aid kit and a cup of tea first. Stay here. I won't be a minute." Charli ran from the barn to the vet's office next door.

Martha stood, grabbed her cane, and looked into the stall at the mother and baby. She laughed as she looked at the new addition. "Sorry, Gracie. I'm not making fun of him but look at those long legs and knobby knees. I know he's going to grow into a handsome fellow, but even you have to agree he's not quite there yet."

Turning to Jared, she said, "He's a fine specimen. Guess Highlander was the right choice for stud. Look at him prance. He already knows he's special." Martha reached into the stall and scratched his nose. "What a beauty you are," she said gazing into his eyes which looked like pools of liquid chocolate. Tears began to spill from Martha's eyes as Gracie came to greet her. She raised her hand to strike them away, then reached up to hug her old friend. Her body shook with the stress and anxiety of the past few months. She buried her face in the horse's neck and allowed the tears to flow.

Grace nickered and comforted Martha as only a best friend could. Sobs subsiding, Martha reached into her pocket for a slice of apple. She held out her hand to the horse. Amazing Grace took the treat with her lips and crunched the fruit with her teeth. She then turned her head and nudged Martha to lick away the salt from her benefactor's cheek.

1

Martha laughed. "Old cupboard love," she smiled as she kissed the horse's nose. Weary, but content now the storm of tears had passed, Martha sat back down on the hay to wait for Charli. Jared said nothing but sat with his grandmother and held her hand. She put her head on his shoulder, serenity softening her body.

Within a few minutes, Charli returned holding a tea tray with tea, biscuits and the first aid kit. She placed it on a bale of hay beside her grandmother.

Jared rose. "I'll leave you two ladies for a little while. If you get tired, Gran, have Charli take you back to the house for a rest. I'll come by later and tell you what I've found." He turned and left the barn.

Charli picked up the antiseptic and cleaned Martha's wound.

"I've been watching our boy while you were gone. Have you figured out a name for him yet?" Martha asked.

"No. I want to get to know him better and let him tell me his name. I've seen him racing around the small paddock. He kicks up his heels and gambols in sheer joy. Then there's those markings."

"My granddaughter, the horse whisperer."

They chuckled together while Charli bandaged her grandmother's arm. When she finished, the two sat in camaraderie drinking their tea and chatting about the ranch. About twenty minutes later, Jared returned.

"What did you find?"

"Not much. There are a bunch of old tires stacked beside the shed at the top of the hill. Don't see how, but the tire pile had fallen over. One must have come loose and rolled down the slope."

"Odd. It's the third peculiar incident that's happened lately. Nothing I can put my finger on, but unnerving."

"What incidents?"

"The small fire in the tack room. Then the fence coming down. Now this. Could be coincidences, I suppose."

"Oh, those incidents. What are you thinking?"

2

"It's all stuff which could be innocent enough, but I'm uneasy. They all happened after those land developers came nosing around. Think I'm being paranoid?"

"Gran, you are the least paranoid person I know. I'll poke around. See what I can find. May be nothing, but if things don't feel right to you, it's worth investigating."

"Do you think we should tell the police?"

"Not yet. We don't have anything to tell them. Only some vague suspicions."

"Ok but be careful. Got an itch between my shoulder blades and I don't like it."

Chapter Two

S ix months later, Martha tucked up in bed, reminisced about the episodes. She picked up her new will and looked at it again. What if they weren't coincidences? What if someone…?

There was a faint knock on the bedroom door. "Mother Bancroft, are you asleep?"

Startled at the sound, she called, "Come in."

Vanessa opened the door and peeked around it. "I saw your light and thought you might like a hot toddy."

"Why, thank you, Vanessa. I thought you and Drew left."

Vanessa placed a mug on the nightstand. The bed sagged as she sat on the edge and took Martha's hands in hers. "I got Andy to turn around and come back. I'm sorry for his temper earlier. It wasn't right to speak to you like that. Are you okay?"

"I'm fine but are you all right? I noticed at supper you didn't eat much. A couple of times you were frowning at Drew. Then, your outburst and running from the room. Not like you. What's going on?"

Vanessa looked down. A tear slipped from her eyes, curved down her cheek and plunked on their joined hands. "Andy's making me mad. Oh, he's happy to show me off to his hoity-toity pals. They call me a 'trophy wife' as if I'm stupid. It hurts my feelings. If I say anything, he laughs it off telling me to go shopping or get my hair done. He never stands up for me either when Adele or Percy are mean. I don't know what to do."

"What do you want to do? Leave him?"

"No. Not yet anyway. I love him. I'd rather try to work it out, but I need some things to change. I also want to see what you're going to do with the ranch. I've been listening to Jared and Charli and the plans sound wonderful. I love animals. I was hoping I'd be able to help somehow." Her face lit up with a smile and there was a longing in her

4

eyes. Martha didn't have the heart to discourage her, but the thought of Vanessa and the disasters which always seemed to follow in her wake were too much for her to think about tonight. Then again, she said she might leave Drew. Wasn't a divorce between them what Martha always wanted? Somehow, that speculation wasn't as gratifying as she thought it would be.

"We'll see what we can do."

Vanessa leaned over and gave the older woman a kiss on the cheek. "Goodnight, Mother. Sleep well." She got up and started to leave the room. As her hand reached for the doorknob, Martha called her back. Her face set in determination, she said, "Vanessa, can you do me a favor?"

Vanessa turned back to her mother-in-law. "Sure. Whaddya want?"

"I need you to sign some papers. I'll sign them first. Then you to sign them to say it's my signature. All right?"

"Sure."

Martha reached for her pen, picked up the will, and signed her name and the date. Handing the pen and paper to Vanessa, she said, "Sign on the line here," pointing to the page, "and add the date. Right. Thank you. You have taken a load off my mind. Promise me you won't tell anyone what you've done. I don't want the others to know - especially Drew."

"But..."

"Please. Tell no one. Promise?"

"Okay, but I don't like keeping things from Andy."

"I know, but it's important. I'll explain everything tomorrow. I need to make him understand why I've done what I've done."

"I promise," Vanessa said exhaling a breath of surrender.

"Thank you," said Martha laying back against the pillows.

Vanessa handed back the pen and signed will, kissed her cheek and left the room. Martha put the documents into the envelope and resealed it. She rose from her bed, hobbled to the fireplace, and got down on her creaking knees. Her hands reached out and pulled the grate forward and placed it to the side of the hearth. Using the shovel utensil, she scooped the ash into a bucket, exposing the tiles beneath. She lifted the large center tile, revealing a hidden safe. Bobby had installed it in their bedroom years ago. After opening the latch, she placed the documents inside and closed the door, spinning the dial to lock it. It was over and done!

She replaced the tile, ash and grate and walked to the ensuite to wash her hands. Her steps unsteady, she shuffled to the bed and climbed in. Reaching for her toddy, she took a sip. A smile curved her lips upward as the warm drink slid down her throat. She snuggled down under the covers. As she continued to savor the beverage, she thought about the signed will and the day ahead. A giant weight lifted from her shoulders. Taking another swallow, her body relaxed and become languid, as if she were floating. She tried to think but couldn't quite remember what was troubling her. Her heart sped up. Alarmed, she gasped for air. Chaotic scenes appeared and disappeared in front of her. She tried to focus on her right hand. Disembodied, it floated away. Lethargic, she let go of the mug. She watched as it tumbled through the air and spilled its contents onto the bedding. Slipping into darkness, Martha Bancroft tumbled into the vast abyss of the unknown.

Chapter Three

Zeus, the tiny Yorkie, was snoring, curled up in his usual spot on the bed. His silver fur, illuminated by a moonbeam shining through the open drapes, rose and fell with his breathing. A gust of wind snapped the curtain. His ears perked up. Hackles raised, the little dog sat up, stared at the darkest part of the room, and growled. Martha stood in the deep shadows.

"Hush, Zeus. It's only me."

Tail thumping, he lay back down.

"What am I doing out of bed?" Martha queried as she walked toward her pet. After a few steps, she stopped. No pain! The burning sensation, like a white-hot blade stabbing her in the small of her back, was gone. Martha looked down. Strange. No cane. She wiggled her leg. Not even a twinge. She took few more steps and stopped. She giggled. Gone were the throbbing aches which had been her constant companions for years. Stretching her arms wide, she danced and whirled around the room. A miracle. Her miracle. She came to a halt. Uneasiness slithered its way into her consciousness. Her body felt different - more buoyant and agile. She felt different.

"Odd."

She contemplated her surroundings. Above the bed hung the Monet she and Bobby picked up in Rome on their second honeymoon. Down two steps, the fireplace and sitting area held her recliner. She scanned all the familiar knickknacks and treasures collected over the years. Definitely her bedroom. Was she dreaming? Her eyes stopped roaming and focused on a strange bulge under the bed covers where she usually slept. Guarded, she drew near to see an elderly woman lying in her spot. Brinicles of ice crystallized within her. She tried to scream, but no sound came. Forcing herself to move closer, Martha stared at the stranger. The woman lay still, eyes and mouth partially open. She was wearing one of Martha's flannel night gowns and a mug had fallen from her outstretched hand. The liquid it contained had spilled and seeped into the bedding. Studying the face, she gasped as recognition registered. These were the features in every recent photo of her, the visage she stared at every day in the mirror. Familiar, yet different.

It didn't make sense. What was happening to her? She plunked down on the edge of the bed, jumping up again as she realized her body made no depression in the mattress. Cautiously, she sat once more. She lifted her hands in front of her face. Twisting them this way and that, she tried to touch her cheeks, but couldn't feel anything. She looked again at the body in the bed. Martha leaned over to close the eyes, but her hand went right through the skull. She jerked back. "What the…?"

Whining, Zeus crawled to her on his belly. She tried to stroke his velvety ears but could no longer feel their softness. "Oh no, no." With a sinking feeling, she stifled a cry. Was she dreaming or… dead? "Must be a nightmare."

She rose and paced the room. "This must be a cosmic joke. Look at me. Sprawled in a soggy bed dressed in my old comfy jammies. I can't let any of them see me like this. I must wake up."

Determined, she strode back to the bed and reached out to shake herself awake, but, as before, her hands went right through the body. She couldn't grasp anything. Panic like an icy waterfall flooded her being. Death couldn't visit tonight! She screamed, sparks from her dream body exploding into the room. "No. This can't be happening. Not now. Wake up, Martha. Wake up, you silly old fool."

Zeus laid his head on his paws, deep brown eyes watching his mistress. His body trembling, he whined. Martha looked at her companion. Her beloved boy. Frustration, anger, and dismay all fought for pre-eminence.

"It's all right, Sweetie. Mommy's right here. Oh, my God, what will happen to you? I can't leave you alone. Not a dream. I'm dead! What

the hell happened?"
    Zeus raised his head and howled.

Chapter Four

Wandering to the library in search of a drink, Jared opened the door. His eyes widened when he found a lamp glowing and Adele seated in one of the overstuffed, upholstered chairs. She looked up as her nephew walked in.

"I couldn't sleep worrying about what your grandmother said she is going to do. You knew about this?"

"Yes, Aunt Adele," he said as he strolled to the credenza and poured himself a drink. Sauntering over to the fireplace, he leaned against it and crossed his legs at the ankles.

"How are you involved? Don't bother denying it. As the ranch vet, I'm guessing you'll be in charge."

"Of the animals, yes."

"You get the lot and there's nothing for me or Percy. He's as much her grandson as you are. I've always known she doted on you more than Percy, but this is appalling. You have no right to take everything away from us! My Eddy was the eldest brother. If Eddy hadn't died, he would be inheriting the family fortune, and this house would be mine. Percy would be next in line. You know it's true. You can't take away our inheritance."

"First, Aunt Adele, I won't even inherit the amount you're getting. Grandma is using her own investment money for the renovations and new buildings. The Foundation she mentioned will be run by a Board of Directors, not me. Any money left will go into an investment fund to help take care of everything. Even then, we'll require some fund raising. I'll be worse off than you, but I happen to agree with Grandma. A sanctuary for unwanted horses is a terrific way to invest her money and build her legacy. But I'd much rather have her here than any of her money."

"Ha. Being here with her every single day? I'm sure you'll find a way to squirm a lot of the funds your way."

Jared put his fingers to his forehead and rubbed the furrow between his brows. "Not everyone is as interested in money and status as you are."

"Don't be ridiculous. People pretend they have no interest in money when they're rich. Well, I've been poor and it's awful. I'm not going back there. I've had to fight and scrape my way here and I won't let you or anyone else take what's mine. Percy was born a Bancroft, and he has every right to his father's legacy."

"You will always have Uncle Edward's share of the estate. If the company is successful, you will be too."

"But the house and grounds are worth a fortune. If she would sell, we could have much more."

Jared took a large swallow of brandy. "This conversation is getting us nowhere. I'm sorry Percy didn't have his father around when he was younger. He might have made something of himself."

"What do you mean 'made something of himself'? There's nothing wrong with Percy. He's always been a delicate child. I did the best I could. And he had your grandfather."

"I guess so, but you avoided visiting as often as you could, didn't you? Looked like you had some beef with Grandpa, so Percy didn't get to share much time with him."

"Well, Robert was not like my Eddy at all. He was a very controlling man and hard on Percy. Why, he wanted him to do all sorts of physical chores which were not at all suitable. I remember one day; Percy came back into the house exhausted and shaking. His Grandfather made him shovel out the horse stalls and put fresh hay down. The poor boy was stoic and did what he could, but it was all too much for him. I had him take a warm bath and then sent him straight to bed for a much-needed rest. It was the last straw. After that, I chose to limit our visits."

"I remember. We were all sent to muck out the stalls. Percy was fooling around in the loft instead of helping. He took all the pitchforks

11

up there and was pretending to toss the hay down. His fingers slipped and one of the forks came flying toward us. It landed right next to Charli, almost hitting her. Percy was white and shaking. He kept hollering, 'It was an accident.' He climbed down the ladder and ran to the house. Charli started crying. 'He could have hurt me,' she said. She was shaking, so I put my arms around her for comfort. We decided not to tell on him as he looked scared. We didn't think he'd try anything similar again. About an hour later we saw him sneaking out of his bedroom and running into the forest."

Adele's face flushed a bright red. Her eyes squinted with menace. "What a dreadful lie. He did no such thing. I never did like to bring him here. You were always telling tales and getting him into trouble. He didn't need any of you. He didn't need anyone but me."

"Really?"

"Yes, really. He's grown up to be a very respectable young man."

"Okay. If you say so. As I said earlier, Grandma has a right to do as she wishes with the land. She has always had a kind heart and wants to help those beautiful animals in any way she can. I'm sure, if he wants, I could find Percy a place here to work and earn his own money."

"You're just like her! A soft touch for anyone with a sob story. You've always been jealous of Percy because he isn't like the rest of you. He is an artist. He would die working on a smelly farm. He's much too delicate."

"Really?"

"You…you impertinent puppy! Thank goodness, the will isn't signed yet. Hopefully, we can talk some sense into your grandmother in the morning. I refuse to stay here and listen to your insults any longer. I will retire to my room." Adele stood and straightened her dress. She was about to make a grand exit when Percy peeked around the door.

"There you are Mother. I was up to our room, but you weren't there. What are you doing up at this hour? Are you all right?" he asked as he strolled to her side.

"My mind was whirling with all the nasty things your grandmother

12

said tonight, so I came down here to get a little something to help me sleep."

"Grandmother was quite out of line. I was shocked and disappointed. Although some of us seemed to do all right out of the whole ordeal. Eh, cousin?" he sneered. Turning, his hooded eyes bored into Jared like two deadly daggers.

Jared placed his glass on the mantle and pushed himself away from the fireplace. Fists clenched at his sides; he approached Percy. "You have a problem with our grandmother, Cousin?"

"Yes. Seems some of us are sucking up to the old lady to get her fortune."

"Maybe if some of us would man up and work for a living, he wouldn't be left out when any goodies rolled around."

"Are you saying I'm not a man?"

"You said it. I didn't."

"Why you—" Percy rushed toward Jared his hands outstretched.

Jared sidestepped his cousin. Percy whizzed past him, tripped over the carpet, and fell face first into a chair. He pushed himself up and was about to attack his nemesis again when they heard an odd sound. Everyone froze in place.

"There it is again. What on earth is that wretched racket?" asked Adele.

"Sounds like Zeus. Why's he howling?" replied Percy.

"I don't know, but it can't be good," exclaimed Jared as he ran to the door and flung it open.

Chapter Five

Martha heard the commotion of her family. The running footsteps. The pounding on her door. She retreated to the corner of her bedroom and watched as the door crashed open.

Jared was the first to enter. Zeus stood in the middle of the bed howling. Jared rushed over and stopped. In front of him lay his grandmother, her body rigid, eyes half closed, her mug tipped over, its contents staining the duvet.

"Grandma."

Andrew Bancroft, his father, came in behind him. "Zeus shut up!" he yelled.

The tiny animal dropped to the bed and lay shivering. Vanessa ran past Andrew and picked up the little dog who whimpered and snuggled into her body. "It's all right, baby. I've got you."

Thomas Winslow, the family lawyer, walked over to the bed. Martha watched as he took in the scene and reached for his cell. While calling 911, he did a quick scan of the room, looking at her bedside table and checking her bookshelves.

"What's he doing? Looking for the will, I'll bet. Good luck with that," Martha muttered to herself.

Adele and Percy were the last ones to enter the room. Adele took one look at her mother-in-law and started to wail.

"Mother Bancroft! Oh! I'm going to faint." She placed her hand on her forehead and started to slump to the floor. Percy caught her, calling out "Mother, Mother!"

Leave it to Adele to make a scene. What Ed saw in her I'll never know.

Tom turned and looked at the small group. "The ambulance is on its way. I suggest we adjourn to the living room and wait for them."

"Good idea," said Percy. "They'll be able to help her."

"I'm afraid Mrs. Bancroft's beyond help."

"What? No, you can't be right," said Jared. "She was fine – a little tired from all the excitement. We were going to discuss the plans for the renovations tomorrow. Gran, Gran, wake up." He reached out to shake her when Tom stopped him.

"Don't touch the body, Jared."

"Why?"

"We shouldn't touch anything 'til the paramedics have seen her. C'mon let's go."

The lawyer put his arm on Jared's shoulder and led him out of the room.

Vanessa, carrying Zeus, strode past Andrew. Tears staining her cheeks, she took one last look at her mother-in-law and hurried out of the room.

Percy helped his mother stand and escorted her from the room. Adele could be heard wailing the whole way down the hall. "Oh, this is terrible. I will need to call Dr. Fitzhugh. I'm not sure my nerves are up to taking this kind of upset. How dreadful. Someone should have escorted her to her room, although, I'm much too weak to be climbing up and down those stairs. My heart wouldn't take it. Anyway, one of you younger people should have been with her."

Martha watched as one by one they left the room. Andrew was the last to go. He walked to the bed and looked down at the still body that had once been his mother. Martha could read the emotions etched on his face. A mixture of horror, sadness, and anger were all there. He stood silent for what seemed like an eternity, then turned and strode out of the room. *Oh, my boy. What happened to us?* The soft click of the door latch sealed the tomb of the family matriarch.

Chapter Six

An icy chill swept over Martha. Zeus. Jared. Charli. All those she loved. "I'm sorry," she sobbed.

She moved to follow them, but a small orb of light, bouncing around the room, distracted her. Her energy sizzled. "What on earth…?" Martha backed away, stopped, and then approached, caution controlling every step. The orb hung in the air in front of her. It had some sort of intelligence and be staring at her. How she didn't know, but she could sense it. Martha watched fascinated as the orb began to dance around. She stiffened her resolve and called out. "Enough of this nonsense. Is someone here?"

"Yes."

"Show yourself."

The ball of light transformed into an androgynous human figure made of light.

"That better?"

"Will this nightmare never end? Who the hell are you?"

"Call me Gladys."

"What are you… an angel or something?"

"Or something."

"Great. NOW I've got an 'or something'. Where were you a few hours ago? How come you didn't stop me from dying?"

"Oh, suck it up, Princess. We all die. You're dead. Finito. Let's go."

"Go? Where? What for?"

"What do you mean 'where?' What's wrong with you? How come you didn't come home when you left your body?"

"Whoa. What are you talking about?"

"You were supposed to come to the light when your soul left your body. When you didn't show up as expected, I was sent to get you. We're all waiting for you. We need to go."

"Who are the 'we' you're talking about?"

"Our soul group. You know. The group of us all working on the same stuff? Our team. We help each other grow and evolve when we come to Earth. Who incarnates with you and who stays behind to watch over you is all decided before you're born. I stayed behind this time. The whole group's been learning through your life challenges. You don't remember?"

"No. Everything's a bit fuzzy right now."

"Hmmm. I didn't see your actual death. What happened?"

"I don't know. I went to bed and the next thing I knew; I was out here, and my body was still lying on the bed."

"Well, it doesn't really matter now. We need to go. Everyone is waiting."

"Well, they can bloody well wait."

"We've got to go NOW."

"Then go. I didn't ask you here. I don't have to go, do I?"

"No. It's your choice. Everything is a choice. Free will and all. Even this. But please don't stay. The rest of us are depending on you."

"I'm staying 'til I find out what happened to me."

"We need you home."

"No."

Gladys held up her hands in submission. "Alright," she said. "Then I'm waiting with you."

"You don't have to."

"Yes, I do. It's important I get you home."

Martha shook her head as if to clear her thoughts. "This is all very confusing. By the way, how come I look like I did before I died, but when you first showed up, you were a ball of light and then morphed into looking human? What's with that?"

"How to explain…. Think of your car. Before you bought it, you looked at several different makes and models until you found one that suited your needs. You were not your car. You owned and operated it

17

for a while. When it had served its purpose, you got a new one. Same thing. A human body is something you choose, like a car. While on earth it's for your use and when life's over, you leave it and move on. You weren't your car and you're not your body. Although right now you're still identifying with it. Everything is pure energy. As energy, you can change your structure into anything you want."

"Give me a break. I just died."

"It's not the first time."

"Really? Have I been a ghost before?"

"Don't know. Usually, the souls in our group go straight to the light, but you decided to stay behind this time. Since you haven't been home yet, your power is a little bit different than mine. See if you can change into a ball."

Martha concentrated. Before long she became a glowing globule like the pieces inside of a lava lamp.

"Cool."

Bobbing around the room, her structure kept changing. A vertical glob stretched to a horizontal sausage shape, then a huge round bubble and finally a shimmering bead of light which shot sparks like fireworks.

Martha laughed. "Woo hoo. It's like taking off your bra at the end of a hard day! I'm free."

"Oh goody! Glad you're having fun. Well since we're on a roll here, and you're not going to come with me, how about we go down to the living room and spy on your relatives?"

"Won't they see us or hear us?"

"Nope. If you notice, we aren't communicating with a voice. We don't have voice boxes anymore. They can't hear us. We'll change shape to be as unobtrusive as possible. You always said you wanted to be a fly on the wall. Now's your chance."

Chapter Seven

Martha and Gladys, cloaked as tiny spheres of light, took a position high in the corner of the drapes near the window. Even if they were spotted, the viewer would think they were reflections or glare spots. The small company could hear sirens getting closer. Martha watched as Tom left the group to open the front gates after which he rejoined the family. Vanessa was in a chair holding Zeus. When he saw the lights enter the room, he began to bark.

"Vanessa! Get that mutt outta here," shouted Andrew.

Martha's anger bubbled up and she turned her focus on her son. Gladys noticed a crystal vase on the table next to Andrew started to teeter.

"Get hold of yourself. You're making the vase rock with your anger."

"Me? I moved the vase?"

"Apparently."

"Hot damn. Can I make it explode?"

"Probably."

"Cool. Wonder what else I can do."

Gladys barked. "Get us in trouble. That's what."

Vanessa cradled the little dog closer to her body. She stood, strode out of the living room, and headed toward the library.

"Follow her," said Martha.

Trailing close behind, they watched Vanessa enter the study and walk over to Zeus's bed near the fireplace. Crouching down, she placed him in it, all the while stroking his fur and whispering to him. "Shh, baby. You mustn't make a noise or Andy will be angry. Here's your own special spot. Don't worry. I'll take care of you no matter what Andy says. You're my sweet boy, aren't you?"

"She's such a nice woman," said Gladys.

"Zeus has always loved her," Martha said in a wistful voice. "I hope Drew will let her keep him. It would be good for both."

"And you didn't trust your dog's instinct?"

Martha sniffed. "Just because Zeus loves her doesn't mean I think she's right for my son."

Soothed by the gentleness of Vanessa's voice, Zeus gave one final woof, then relaxed and fell asleep. Vanessa rose and left the room, her unseen entourage following behind. She was in the foyer as an ambulance from the Durham Region EMS arrived. Waiting until they entered the house, she directed them to Martha's room and then went to join the rest of the family.

"Let's go with the paramedics. I'd like to see what they think," said Martha.

Entering Martha's room, the paramedics walked over to the bed and examined the body. Seeing nothing unusual about the lividity or rigor mortis, one of the EMT's packed up their gear, while the other filled out the endless paperwork involved in a home death.

"Anti-climatic or what?" hissed Martha.

"I dunno. This is fun. I've never hung around after a death," said Gladys.

"Easy for you to say. It's not your dead body dressed in old jammies, sprawled in the most undignified position on a bed, having a bunch of strangers poke and prod you. If I weren't already dead, I'd die of embarrassment. Nothing much to see here. Let's follow them downstairs and find out what's going on."

The duo watched as the paramedics carried their gear back to the EMS vehicle but stopped as a police cruiser drove up to the house. Two uniformed officers from Central West Division got out.

"What's up, Matt?" asked the driver.

"Old lady appears to have died not too long ago. Rigor is settling in. She doesn't appear to have been moved."

"Who's he calling an old lady?" muttered Martha.

"Anything look suspicious?"

"There is a mug tipped over onto the bed. Could be nothing. Probably a heart attack. The coroner will need to call it."

"Thanks, fellas. We'll take over from here." Pulling out their notebooks, both officers wrote down the time they arrived and the conversation with the paramedics. They walked up to the house, Martha and Gladys staying close. Entering the hall, the officers saw a lone man standing by the door.

"Trust Drew to be front and center," muttered Martha.

"Who's in charge, here?" asked one of the officers.

"I am," replied Andrew. "My name is Andrew Bancroft, the deceased's son."

"Officer Carlos Sanchez and this is my partner Officer Jimmie Chan. Mind telling me the name of the deceased?"

"Mrs. Martha Bancroft, owner of the estate."

"Who else is here?"

"The rest of the family and Mother's attorney."

"Where are they?"

"In the living room."

"Fine. Mr. Bancroft, I suggest you join the others. I will need to call this in. The coroner should be along shortly."

"Coroner? Is that necessary? I can call the funeral parlor."

"Routine, Mr. Bancroft. The coroner must be called on all home deaths to pronounce the person deceased and sign the death certificate."

"The coroner. Interesting. Wonder what he'll discover," said Martha.

"Alright, Officer. I'll join the others." Andrew went into the living room while the two police officers stood at the front door. Officer Sanchez called his sergeant and soon an unmarked car with two men in suits pulled up to the front steps. Detectives Ian MacKellar and Joseph Surrey exited the car.

"Hey, Carlos. Hey Jimmie. What going on?"

"Hey, Mac. Death of an elderly woman during the night. The family and the woman's attorney are in the living room."

"Her attorney, eh? Interesting. Wonder what he's doing here? It's now one-thirty. Mark it in your notebooks. Carlos, bring the attorney out here for a little chat and then make sure none of the rest of them try to leave. Jimmie, guard the front door. Make sure no one comes in or out except the coroner."

Officer Sanchez went to get Tom and bring him to the detective. After the introductions, Detective MacKellar said, "I understand the deceased has been identified as Mrs. Martha Bancroft. Can you tell me who else is in the house and why they're here?"

"Certainly, Detective. There's myself; Martha's son Andrew and his wife, Vanessa; Mrs. Adele Bancroft, widow of Martha's eldest son Edward, and her son Percy; and Dr. Jared Bancroft, Andrew's son. We were all invited for dinner by the deceased."

"Dr. Bancroft?"

"Yes. He is a Doctor of Veterinary Medicine and the vet for the ranch."

"A regular Friday night family dinner?"

"It's not a regular occurrence, but Mrs. Bancroft wanted her family here so she could discuss some important family business."

"Which would be?"

"Her plans for the property and the contents of a new will."

"Right. What time was dinner?"

"Around seven."

"Everything alright?"

"Yes, everything was normal. After we finished, Mrs. Bancroft asked we all meet in the library at nine as she wished to discuss something of importance. She then went to her room."

"Then what?"

"She came down about eight forty-five and we went into the library to wait for the rest of the family. They all arrived at nine."

"What was discussed?"

"Mrs. Bancroft explained she would be changing her will and then outlined the new distributions of the estate. It was a trying meeting and she decided to retire for the night. The rest of us milled around for a while and then went to bed. We were awakened in the middle of the night by the dog howling."

"Was the family in agreement over the contents of the will?"

"Ummm, no. All the family, except Jared, were distressed. Andrew was quite upset and left the house along with his wife, Vanessa."

"What time did they leave?"

"Around ten. The reading didn't take long. It would only have been an hour, maybe a little longer, before Andrew and Vanessa left. Mrs. Bancroft went to bed eleven. She talked to her grandson Jared and me first, and then went on upstairs."

"What did you talk about?"

"We discussed the renovation plans for the property. The architects presented Mrs. Bancroft with detailed drawings, and she was quite excited about showing them to us tomorrow… umm, well, I guess that would be today."

"No one accompanied her to her room?"

"No."

"Where is the new will now?"

"I don't know. Mrs. Bancroft asked for it along with other papers involved with the transfer of the land."

"Was it signed?"

"Not when she took it upstairs with her."

"Did you see it in the bedroom when you went to investigate why the dog was howling?"

"I didn't."

"You have no idea where it is?"

"No."

"Nothing's been touched in Mrs. Bancroft's room?"

"Not as far as I know."

"Where are the others now?"

"They're all waiting in the front room."

"Fine. You go and remain with them. I'll be there shortly once I've seen the deceased. Where is her room?"

"Up the staircase to the left. Mrs. Bancroft's room is at the far end of the hall in the back part of the house."

"Thank you, Mr. Winslow. That's all for now."

"Let's follow the cop," said Gladys.

"Man, I love being a fly on the wall," said Martha.

Tom went back into the living room. Mac mounted the stairs and walked to Martha's room. The spirits saw him walk over to the bed and look at Martha's body. He took out his notebook and noted the time of his visual examination as well as the overturned mug. He rubbed the back of his neck. "Looks okay, but my spidey senses are tingling," he muttered to himself.

Chapter Eight

Leaving the bedroom, the trio descended the stairs as the coroner and forensic team arrived. Dr. Cecilia Walsh was a striking blonde with grey eyes.

"Hey, Mac. What's up?"

"Hi, Doc. Death of an old woman. We need you to pronounce death."

"Here we go again. Old woman! Watch it, buddy," muttered Martha.

"Oh, give it up," spat Gladys. "You were old! Sheesh. Keep quiet so I can hear what they're saying."

"Hrmmph," said Martha, turning back to the pair in front of them.

"No problem. Anything amiss?" asked the coroner.

"Don't think so, but I've got that itchy feeling. Old lady gets her family together to talk about changing her will and a few hours later, she's dead. This is a prominent family in the area. I prefer to err on the side of caution. See what you think, but I'm leaning toward an autopsy just to be sure."

"An autopsy? Why would he want an autopsy? Wonder what he's thinking," said Martha.

"Maybe it wasn't a heart attack?" answered Gladys.

"What else could have happened?" mused Martha.

"Okay. Let's see what we've got."

Mac led the way to Martha's room. While Dr. Walsh examined the body, Mac looked again at the mess on the covers. "Bag the mug and blanket, Sam," he instructed one of the team. "I'd like to know about the stain."

"Sure thing, Mac."

Mac wandered into the bathroom and opened the medicine cabinet. He put on his gloves and picked up the medicine containers placed on the shelves. He wrote down the contents, dosage, and instructions in his notebook. He checked the garbage pail and assorted items on the counter. Returning to the room, the doctor looked up.

"Find anything interesting?"

"Nope. A couple of prescriptions but nothing out of the ordinary for a seventy-five-year-old."

"Like you said, we need to be thorough with this one. Full autopsy it is. I'm done here. I'll call for the body van and get them to take her to Toronto. I'm outta town this weekend. I'll schedule it for Monday morning and let you know what I find. The toxicology report will take a bit longer, but I'll put a rush on it."

"Thanks, Doc. Sounds great. I'm going downstairs to question the family. Would you mind sticking around for a bit? I like to talk to you after the prelims. Shouldn't take more than an hour."

"No problem. Where would you like me to wait?"

"Why don't we go downstairs and see if we can get you a coffee in the kitchen?"

"That works. I've got a couple of things to finish up on my laptop. Come get me when you're done."

"These two seem to know each other. Wonder if they've worked together before. Sounds competent. Not like some idiots I know. I like her," said Martha, satisfaction tinging her voice.

Mac and Dr. Walsh, with their attendants, descended the stairs and spoke to the constables at the door. "The team from the morgue is on their way to pick up the body. I'll be questioning the family. Dr. Walsh will wait in the kitchen. Once I've questioned everyone, they'll be free to go." Turning to Joe he said "God, I hope this is a simple case of death during sleep, but somehow, I don't think so. Let's get this over with."

All eyes turned to the detectives as they entered the living room. Martha and Gladys made their way to the drapes and hid in the folds.

"What's going on, Detective?" asked Andrew.

"Please, sit down Mr. Bancroft."

Andrew frowned and took a seat on his mother's usual chair.

"Hmph. Look at the King of the Hill," snorted Martha.

"Shhh. I want to hear what they're saying," hissed Gladys.

"My name is Detective Ian MacKellar, and this is my partner, Detective Joseph Surrey. I'm sorry to inform you that Mrs. Martha Bancroft was pronounced dead at four-thirty this morning by the coroner. Mrs. Bancroft's body will be transported to Toronto for an autopsy. When the forensic pathologist has completed her duties, Mrs. Bancroft will be released to the funeral home for burial."

"What?" shouted Andrew, leaping from the chair. "Why is an autopsy required? She was an elderly lady who died in her sleep! This is an outrage. Mother would be mortified. Tom, do something!"

"Listen to him. He has no idea what I want. Sit down, you pompous ass," groaned Martha.

"An autopsy? Mother wouldn't like that at all," cried Adele. "The indignity!"

The family members all began shouting.

"Please, everyone! Settle down. Mrs. Bancroft was seventy-five and in apparent good health. The coroner would like a definitive cause of death and an autopsy will, hopefully, answer the question. In the meantime, I would like to ask you all a few questions. Is there a private room we could use for interviews?"

"There's a small sunroom through there," replied Andrew, pointing to a door beside the picture window. "Mother likes – I mean liked, to sit out there to read and relax. It has a couple of chairs and a small coffee table. Will that do?"

"Excellent, Mr. Bancroft. I'll get set up and Detective Surrey will call your names one by one. Once I have questioned you, you'll be free to go."

Chapter Nine

M ac walked to the door and entered the room. A light scent of lavender greeted his nose. The muted lighting, soft pastel colours, polished oak floors and walls made of glass overlooking landscaped gardens gave an aura of warmth and coziness. Two comfortable tub chairs and matching ottomans were placed on an area rug of thick plush. Mac stopped, filled his lungs with air through his nostrils and let it escape with a sigh from his mouth. The stress in his neck and shoulders sank through his body and out the bottoms of his feet to be buried into the rug. A small wood stove tucked away in the corner provided warmth on a chilly day. He could understand why this might be the lady's favorite room. Mac lifted a small table and placed it in the center of the room. Picking up the chairs, he put them on opposite sides of the table.

Turning to his partner, he said, "Bring in Mr. Andrew Bancroft, Joe."

Andrew was ushered into the sitting room, with his mother and Gladys following along. The spirits took up positions over by the wood stove.

"Have a seat Mr. Bancroft. Now, what time did you arrive at your mother's last evening?"

"My wife and I were the first to arrive at about six forty-five."

"Just your mother was home?"

"No. Her attorney Thomas Winslow was with her in the library."

"Wish you could see what happened," whispered Martha to Gladys.

"We can. I have an idea."

"Really?"

"Yes. I can produce a hologram showing the time when the family arrived. We'll become part of the scene and able to feel everyone's emotions, but we are only observers. Like now, no one will be able to see or hear us."

"Neat. Let's do it."

Gladys concentrated her energy and a whirling hologram circled in front of them. The scene displayed was of Martha earlier in the evening, sitting in the library. The spirits joined the tableau. All the emotions in the room washed over Martha in a torrent and she reeled back at the onslaught.

Martha sat in her wingback chair in the library sipping tea. Frowning, she noticed crumbs on the jacket of her blue-gray denim pantsuit. She plucked them off and put them in the saucer. Wouldn't do for any of them to see her less than perfect. She'd much rather be in her jeans and a sweatshirt, but tonight, especially, she must appear at her best and strongest. White hair styled in a perfect bob, check. Makeup meticulously applied, check. Dressed for the occasion, check. The ideal picture of the "Matriarch". She'd come a long way from her mother's tiny home and the handmade clothes she wore when she was a child. Now, she had to play her part and prepare for the invasion of her family. She leaned forward to address her attorney. As usual, he was pacing the room. *Such a worry wart for someone as young as he is. Wish his father were still around.*

"Should be an amusing evening eh, Tom?"

He stopped in front of her chair. "Are you sure you want to go through with this?"

"Of course. You're sure they're all coming?"

"They all replied to my secretary with a yes."

She smiled at her attorney. "Good."

Tom frowned at his client. "I really don't think this is a good idea, Martha. The family will be furious with your plans. It's not worth the risk of alienating them at this stage of your life."

"Don't be ridiculous. It's my property and my money. I will do what I think is best for me. They all have ample to sustain them. I won't be deterred from this, Tom, regardless of what you or they think."

"As you say. It's your money, but you're taking a big gamble."

Tom continued his pacing while Martha sat back in her chair and gazed around the room. The library of the Bancroft ranch was large, designed as a man cave for the patriarch, Robert. She could still feel him there and, at times, smell his favorite cologne. She felt close to him here, although she was not at all fussy about the dark cherry wood paneling. She'd redo it and brighten up the room. The picture window glistening across from the door gave lot of light. The heavy drapes could be replaced by softer sheers. She'd keep the old banker's desk they picked up at an estate sale on one of their Saturday morning jaunts. Polished to a glistening patina, it was placed in front of the window, facing in, to give Bobby an advantage by casting visitors in a bright light while he was cloaked in shadow. Floor-to-ceiling bookshelves stood on either side of the window and held their favorite reading material. Martha chuckled to herself as she recalled many an evening spent debating the merits of various authors. When the discussion became heated, the desk or the rug in front of the fireplace would become useful for another type of activity.

A large stone fireplace filled the wall to the left of the entryway, a conversation pit, including Martha's chair grouped in front of it. A portrait of Bobby hung over the mantle. A liquor cabinet behind the door held crystal decanters of Glen Livet, Belvanie and Remy Martin XO Excellence, plus glasses. A locked humidor, containing half a dozen Davidoff Series Mille 3000 panatelas, held priority placement to the left of the glasses. The scents of cream, wood, leather, and nuts permeated the air near the console.

Stroking Zeus, who was lying in her lap, Martha put her teacup on the side table. Her gnarled hand reached for her cane. Sensing his mistress was about to move, the little dog jumped down to the floor.

Walking over to the fireplace, a lightning bolt of pain sizzled from the small of her back, through Martha's hip and down her right leg. She hissed in air through clenched teeth.

"Let me help you, Martha," called Tom as he hurried toward her.

"No, thank you. I can manage. I'm not in my dotage yet."

Using her cane as an anchor, she could stand for several minutes to gaze, as she often did, on the painting of her husband. The image portrayed a man in his prime. His black hair, cut to touch the collar of his shirt, was peppered with white. Cobalt eyes twinkled from the lined and rugged face of a man who loved the outdoors. With his muscular build and laborer's hands, his looks belied hours spent at a computer. His smile was genuine, but she knew it exuded a power few men would cross. She took a deep breath and felt her heart settle in peace. The portrait never failed to strengthen her. How she loved him.

She walked back to her chair. Placing her cane beside her table, she lowered her body into the plush cushions. She laid her head against the back of the chair as the pain dissipated. Padding along behind, Zeus whimpered. Martha reached down and lifted him onto her lap. He settled in with a huge sigh. Martha caressed his silky fur. "Such a good boy. Mommy loves you to bits," she whispered.

The sound of a key in the lock broke into her reverie as she heard the front door open. Footsteps echoed in the hall. A stocky man in his early fifties with gray, thinning hair came into her view. *Drew. He would be the first one here. Never one to miss out on anything.* She frowned at the flabby jowls and slight paunch which told of his love for fine dining and expensive wine. Dressed in formal attire, he approached Martha and brushed her cheek with his.

"Good evening, Mother. Tom."

"Drew. I'm glad you could come. Is Vanessa with you?"

Andrew frowned. "I do wish you would call me Andrew and yes, Mother, Vanessa is with me, much to your dismay, I suppose. I swear, if you aren't kind to her, I'll leave… summons or not!"

31

What a pretentious idiot. "Don't get into a snit. I'm glad she's joining us. We'll be meeting after dinner and what I have to say is for everyone to hear."

A high-pitched voice echoed in the foyer.

"Arrgh! Stupid rain!"

Recognizing the voice, Zeus flew off Martha's lap and landed on the floor. Nails scrambling on the hardwood, he raced down the hall toward the front door. Yipping, he darted straight to the young woman who had entered the house.

"Zeusie! Where's my precious boy?"

Laughing, Vanessa reached down to pick up the dog and cradle him in her arms. Zeus, tail whirling like a helicopter rotor, snuggled into her, lavishing her face with licks, and making gurgling sounds in his throat. "Stop it, you silly boy," she said giggling. "Behave yourself. You're going to ruin my makeup. C'mon, let's see who's here."

She set him down on the ground. They walked down the hallway and entered the library. Zeus made his way to Martha's chair and curled up at her feet.

"What a dreadful evening. I've nearly ruined my Jimmy Choo's. I just had my hair done, bought this lovely outfit and it decides to rain. Honestly, I think the gods must be against me. Hello everyone. Good evening, Mother Bancroft. Sorry I'm a bit behind, but I left my purse in the car and had to run back for it."

"Of course, you did. Good evening, Vanessa. Your dress is delightful."

"Yes, isn't it?" replied Vanessa. She twirled around in front of them, her long dark tresses making a curtain around her. "Andy said I didn't need a new one for tonight, but I told him I couldn't wear just any old thing to Mother's dinner party, now could I? I had a little shopping spree this afternoon," she giggled. "And look at this matching bag. Isn't it gorgeous? I do love a new bag. Of course, I'm always forgetting them and leaving them somewhere," she said in a soft voice, frowning down at the prized pocketbook. "I do hope I don't forget this one. I love it to

32

pieces."

The girl's head is emptier than a dry well on a sweltering summer day. Nothing but dust inside. "It's a lovely ensemble. I'm glad you could make it."

"Oh, I wouldn't miss it for the world. Andy said you might want to talk about the money you're going to give him and the rest of the family. He told me I could get some new accessories for my dress. A new necklace or bracelet. I like diamonds. If I could find a necklace with sapphires in it as well… mmmm… perfect."

Martha gave a small cough and covered her mouth with her hand. Tom turned away as if to examine a painting on the wall. Andrew clenched his teeth and said, "Not now, Vanessa."

For one millisecond, Vanessa's eyes narrowed as she looked at her husband, then her usual vacant stare returned. She looked around the room. "Where is everyone?"

"Adele and Percy are late, as usual. We should adjourn to the living room for a glass of sherry while we wait for the others to arrive?"

"Wonderful idea, Mother," said Andrew.

Martha picked up her cane and after a small struggle, rose from her chair. "Come along, Zeus," she commanded as she made her way to the door. Vanessa came to her side and gently took her arm. "You look especially nice this evening, Mother Bancroft. I love your pantsuit. It is the perfect color for you. When I was shopping today, I saw a beautiful pair of earrings in the jeweler's downtown that would look stunning with it. We should go shopping…." As their voices faded out, Andrew turned to Tom.

"I'm glad you're here tonight Tom. I've been meaning to get in touch with you about our plans. I met with the developers…."

The two men left the room, Andrew regaling Tom with his next big scheme for the estate.

Chapter Ten

As the hologram faded, Gladys returned them to the room saying, "What a family?"

"You ain't seen nothin' yet, sister," replied Martha. "Wait 'til you meet the rest of them." They turned their attention to Andrew who was still being questioned by Mac.

"How did your mother seem to you?"

"Fine."

"What happened next?"

"We adjourned to the living room for a glass of pre-dinner sherry. Adele and Percy were late. Adele is my brother Edward's widow and Percy is their son. They are the most god-awful, pretentious twits."

"He should talk," muttered Martha. Turning to Gladys she asked, "Want to see our fabulous dinner? Only this time, can we tone down the energy?"

"Sure," answered Gladys. "I'll put a barrier between you and their feelings, so they won't overwhelm you." Gladys pooled her energy, and another hologram took shape. The scene shifted to the living room. It overlooked the circular driveway and iron gates of the front entrance. A quiet, inviting room, decorated in pale mauve with an Aubusson rug woven in the same shades of mauve, darker purples, beige and white covered the floor. The light mauve curtains on the bay window to the right of the entrance opened to reveal a vista of the front lawn with a large ornamental fountain and lush gardens. The window seat contained a small dog bed holding stuffies where Zeus spent many hours on sentry duty. Martha's desk, situated beside the window, afforded her a view of visitors coming up the walk as well as keeping her close to Zeus.

Everyone mingled, chatting with the usual small talk, when the front door opened again, and a whining voice shrilled above the babble.

"Percy, take my coat upstairs to our room. I hope the heat is up. I

34

certainly don't wish to take a chill, especially with all this rain. I do feel as if I have a cold coming on, but I couldn't disappoint the family and not come. It's my duty to be here."

Martha took a deep breath. *Lord give me strength.*

Adele entered the room sniffling. Dressed in an upscale fashion, which, unfortunately did nothing to enhance her faded beauty, she descended on Martha in a cloud of Chanel. Arms outstretched, she grabbed Martha's shoulders, and leaned in to kiss both cheeks. "Mother Bancroft. This dreadful weather! I really shouldn't be out, but then I couldn't refuse such a lovely invitation, now could I? Especially, since everyone else is here. We didn't miss anything, did we?"

Martha winced as she extricated herself from the grip. "Hello, Adele. I'm glad you and Percy could make it. No, you haven't missed a thing. We are waiting on Jared."

Adele looked around the room. Her face had all the fine lines of crinkled tissue paper. To anyone who didn't know her, she would appear as a cherubic maiden aunt, except for the laser beam eyes which now pierced each member of the gathered group.

"Of course, we are," muttered Adele with a smirk. "Couldn't start without the golden boy. Ah, Percy, there you are."

Martha looked up, eyes widening as she watched her grandson glide into the room. *Good heavens. Looks like a bird has built a nest on his chin! And what an outfit.* Percy decked out all in black except for a flamboyant red scarf and beret, pranced over to her chair. Leaning down, he brushed his cheek against hers. Zeus gave a low growl from his position at Martha's feet.

Percy jerked back, scowling at the little animal. "Hello, Grandmother. It's good to see you again."

"Percy, I'm glad you and your mother could make it."

"We were delighted to receive your invitation, weren't we Mother? Although I'm not sure Mother should be out in this weather and I'm missing a private concert by the Maestro," he sniffed, his nose in the air.

35

"But it can't be helped. Family comes first."

Ha. Money comes first, you mean. You both know on which side your bread is buttered.

His long slender fingers patted Martha's hand. He turned and walked toward his mother. Martha's eyes narrowed as she watched Adele whisper in his ear.

Simpering twit. Oh, this is going to be good.

Percy snickered. "Really, Mommy, you are too droll."

Observing them, a frown forming on her brow, Martha asked, "Do you have something you want to share with us, Adele?"

"Oh, no," replied Adele. "I was saying to Percy how nice it was to have the family all together again. It should be a lovely evening."

Martha smirked. *Let's see how you feel when it's over.*

The scene faded and the two spirits were once again in Martha's small room.

Chapter Eleven

Mac continued to question Andrew.

"And after they arrived?"

"We were waiting for my son, Jared. Dr. Jared Bancroft. He's the veterinarian for the ranch. He was performing surgery on one of the horses, so he was late. When he arrived, we made our way into dinner."

"Everything was normal?"

"As normal as it could be in this family."

"Want to see what dinner at the Bancroft's look like?" asked Martha.

"Let's go," replied Gladys.

The scene reopened to show the living room. A man in his early thirties entered from the back of the house. *Jared. Finally. He looks like his grandfather.* Dressed in casual slacks, polo shirt and loafers, he strode over to his grandmother and gave her a hug, kissing her cheek. Martha closed her eyes taking in the scent of him. *He even smells like my Bobby.*

"Hello, Duchess. How are you feeling?" he whispered in her ear.

Martha reached up to return the hug, a smile on her face and a twinkle in her eye.

"Hello, my darling boy. I'm fine. You're looking very handsome tonight. Where's Charli?"

"She's going to stay with Grace. I'll let her know about what's going on later."

"Is Gracie ok?"

"She came through the surgery like the champion she is. Everything's going to be fine."

"What a relief. She's a special gal. By the way, how is your mother?" asked Martha.

"Fine. She sends her love."

Straightening, Jared turned to face the group. "Hello, everyone. Sorry I'm late. Emergency surgery. Lovely night for ducks, eh?" Out of the corner of his eye, he spotted his father. Turning to him, he said, "Hello, Dad. It's good to see you."

Andrew frowned at his son; his lips pursed.

"Everything alright?"

"Now it is. Had a bit of an emergency with Amazing Grace, but everything's fine now."

"Where's your sister?"

"Charli's with Grace. I'll tell her later what's going on here."

"Her name is Charlotte," replied Andrew turning his back on his son. Watching the exchange, a slow anger flamed in Martha's gut. D*rew, you idiot. Why can't you appreciate your children?* She glanced around the room. Adele and Percy were lost in their own weird world and Tom was busy fussing with his briefcase at her desk. Only Vanessa was distressed. By the time Martha blinked, the sadness had left her eyes, and she was smiling.

The group milled around the room chatting, until the cook signaled dinner was ready. Martha nodded.

"Dinner's ready and we don't want it to get cold. Please, everyone, let's go into the dining room. Jared, give me your arm. Zeus, you go to your bed. Good boy. Tom, I would like you to take the seat on my left. The rest of you can sit where you want."

Taking her grandson's arm, Martha was escorted across the hall to the dining room. An expansive Ethan Allen mahogany table held centre place. Martha sat at the head of the table, Jared on her right, Tom on her left. Andrew and Vanessa sat to the left of Tom. Adele and Percy to the right of Jared. A great proponent of encouraging local artisans, Martha decorated the room with paintings, blown glass and metal works from up-and-coming artists who lived close to the estate. One of her favourite pastimes, visiting local art shows to meet the artistic community, had proved valuable with exquisite and unique pieces added to her collection. Once everyone was settled, the meal was served. She watched and listened to their prattle. Vanessa spoke up.

"Where did you get the beautiful blue bowl on the sideboard, Mother?"

"I picked it up at the Port Perry Art in the Park in the summer."

"It's lovely, I thought maybe it came from a museum or one of those exclusive stores downtown."

Adele and Percy snickered. "Silly girl. Have you ever been to a museum of fine art? Their pieces are much finer," said Percy.

"Enough," shouted Andrew. "I'll not have my wife badgered again in this house."

"It's ok, Andy. I'm sure he didn't mean to hurt my feelings."

"No, it's not all right. You are my wife, and this is my home. The least the family could do is show you some respect. Mother, you need to put a stop to this constant ridicule of Vanessa."

"You're right, Drew. Leave the poor girl alone. Understand? Now, who has any news to share with us?"

Adele spoke up. "You'll all be delighted to know I have found a new doctor."

"What happened to Dr. Rose?" asked Martha.

"That quack," Adele bristled. "I told him about my recurring palpitations and how I was having difficulty sleeping. He had the nerve to tell me I was fine, and I should try some warm milk to settle my nerves before I went to bed. Me. Lactose intolerant. I'd be up all night with excruciating stomach pains. I informed him I would be finding another physician who really cared about his patients, and I did. Dr. Weston is a lovely man. So kind. He's ordered several new tests and I'm sure he'll produce a diagnosis in no time," she finished smiling at the group.

Oh, Bobby, help me keep my mouth shut.

Percy spoke up next.

"The Maestro has plans to take a select group of his students on a trip this summer to Austria to visit the birthplace of Mozart. While we are there, we will be touring the various places where Haydn and Beethoven wrote and performed. Ah, to sit in the cafes and absorb the culture of where these men lived. Magnificent. We will be touring for a month. The Maestro has particularly asked for me to join the group. He says my musical skills are increasing at a good rate and he was especially pleased with a little piece I wrote last week. He feels being immersed in the atmosphere where the master's worked will help me enormously."

"We are so excited," exclaimed Adele. "It's quite an honor to be chosen to join this select group. The Maestro thinks highly of Percy's talent." Percy smiled at his mother and patted her hand.

Ha. What talent? Percy's money, more like, thought Martha.

"And how much is this wundertour going to cost?" asked Jared.

"Only a measly twenty thousand. But the benefit! It will be priceless."

Clenching her jaw, Martha pictured her teeth as prison bars holding back the caustic remark threatening to spill out of her mouth. The group talked among themselves as the eating commenced. Martha glanced at Vanessa and noticed she was staring at her plate pushing the food around.

Hmmm. I need to talk to her. We'll find time after dinner.

Jared broke her concentration as he turned to her and asked, "How is Zeus doing with his training?"

"Great. He got his little "visitor" vest and we've taken him to one senior's home already. He loves the old people, and they adore him. It's very gratifying to see the joy he brings them. Last week he…." As their conversation gathered steam, Vanessa's unhappiness seemed to fade.

After dessert, Martha stood up and clinked her glass. "Everyone, please."

The room quieted and all turned their attention to her.

"As you are aware, I invited you here this weekend to discuss a few family matters. For the next hour or so, you may do as you wish, but I

40

want to reconvene in the library at nine o'clock. I'm going to my room to rest until then and I do not wish to be disturbed."

With her pronouncement, she took hold of her cane and, back ramrod straight, marched out of the room. Zeus followed close behind.

Entering her bedroom, Martha walked to her recliner. Zeus trotted over to his bed by the fire and lay down. Her aching body sank into the chair. Nerve endings, raw from inflammation, calmed little by little. Gritting her teeth, she pushed the button allowing the chair to glide to a reclining position. As the pain eased, she thought about her family.

Oh, how I would like to be a fly on the wall downstairs. They'll all be discussing my momentous announcement. Hah... they think they know what I'm planning. Surprise!

Letting her mind wander back in time, she thought of her husband, Bobby. Founder and CEO of Gateway Security, he had been a tech wizard and made a fortune designing home alarm systems in the '70's. They bought a large piece of property in Ashburn, where they raised their two sons, Edward, and Andrew. Ed died in an accident twenty-five years ago and five years ago, Bobby suffered a fatal heart attack. The estate, one hundred acres of prime Ontario farmland, held several large barns and outbuildings. The forty-acre woods enclosed horse trails which threaded throughout the trees. It had been their dream to turn the farm into a high-class ranch, raising quality thoroughbreds for the racing circuit. Until Bobby's company reached a level of success on which they could afford to start building their stable, they rented out the land to local farmers for growing crops. Little by little they built their dream. For the last thirty years, their farm grew and prospered. It had become a household name for producing some of the finest horses in the province. Martha reveled in every minute of the process. With the decline of horse racing in Ontario since the 2012 government funding decision, Martha saw more and more horses sold at auction for the meat industry. Always at the forefront of protests since the '60's, for the past two years, she put her energy into rescuing those unfortunate beasts who found themselves on the chopping block. She may not be able to save all of them, but, by God, she was determined to liberate those she could. As an essential part of her plan, she was redesigning the estate to be a sanctuary for as many reclaimed animals she could. Jared and Charli were on board, and she was excited to begin this new chapter in their lives. Jared was the ranch's vet and, as such, his office was all set up on the property and going smoothly. By next summer, the lavender fields would be producing the abundance of flowers Charli would need to make her infusions, soaps, skin creams and baked goods to help fund the effort. Martha would have a legacy to pass down to future generations. Her work would be well known; the future of the Oak Ridges Moraine secured in her little corner of it, and many animals would be emancipated. Win/win for all.

But was she really being fair to the rest of the family? Drew was her son. Maybe this new will wasn't such a good idea. Could they find a compromise? She just didn't know! On the one hand, she had a son, two daughters-in-law and another grandson who would take the money and waste it in the most appalling manner. Rumor said Drew was all set to sell the property to Fern Glen developers. Sell to that sleazy group?

"Never," said Martha. No. She couldn't give them any more money or control over the fate of the ranch. But he was the only son she had left! A cloud passed in front of the sun, casting the room into shadow. Martha shivered. It reminded her of the day of the fund-raising fair held at the estate in May. What had started out faultless soon took a downturn.

Chapter Twelve

Returning to the sunroom, Gladys said, "Interesting and helpful. I'm beginning to understand why you feel the way you do."

"But you haven't seen that day at the ranch."

"What day at the ranch?" asked Gladys.

"The day of the fund raiser. You need to see it to understand why I acted now."

"Okay. Don't get your knickers in a knot."

Gladys concentrated her energy and went back in time to the day of the fundraiser.

A perfect day in the Durham region. Azure blue skies streaked with wispy cumulus clouds bespoke excellent weather for the festival. Martha paced in her bedroom; her brow puckered in a frown as she mentally checked off her list of 'To Dos' for the day. Dignitaries from the area invited. Notices of the gala published in all the local papers. Flyers posted everywhere. All social media informed, and a posting placed on the new estate website.

A rap on the door broke her reverie. "Come in."

The door opened and Jared stepped into the room.

"Jared. How glad I am to see you."

"I'm here, too," said another voice as Charli stepped out from behind her brother and walked over to hug her grandmother.

"Charli. This is wonderful. I'm glad I have both of you here before everything gets crazy."

"Yup. We're here so you can relax. The weather's perfect. It's going to be a wonderful day. Even Zeus is on his best behaviour."

Martha began pacing again and wringing her hands.

"Grandma, what's wrong?"

"Didn't sleep too well last night. Jumpy. Can't describe it. I feel like Pigpen in the Snoopy comics. Under a dark cloud," she said, a shiver coursing through her body.

Jared went over to his grandmother and put his knuckle under her chin. He lifted it until their eyes met and smiled at her. "Charli and I are here to make sure everything goes smoothly. You're not to worry. C'mon. We want to show you what we've done to the entrance." Martha looked deep into Jared's eyes and a smile formed on her face. She nodded and said, "I'm a silly old fool. You're right. Let's get outta here and show our guests a good time."

Linking arms, the trio marched out of the room and down the stairs, laughter echoing in the hall. Once out the front door, Martha paused and took a long breath in. "Ah. Good country air." Jared and Charli laughed. "Only a hardened horse woman would say that. Can't you hear Aunt Adele? *'Oh, the smell. I know it's giving me a migraine, but since it pleases our dear Mother, I shall just carry on.'* Everyone burst into laughter as they made their way down to the entrance of the estate. There, three trapeze artists were twirling on their perches thirty feet off the ground over the path leading to the house. The walkway went around to the right of the house. There, children, and their parents waited to ride a huge Ferris wheel set up in the corner of the yard. Several plastic swimming pools of varied sizes for visiting dogs dotted the landscape. Behind the house, on the patio, tables and food booths were set up to provide seating and eclectic fare for anyone wanting refreshments. Beyond the food area, a large tent was erected. Inside the tent were rows of tables and chairs. A stage, erected at the front of the tent, showcased a chamber orchestra playing classical music. There would be a variety of performers throughout the day. Exiting the tent by another opening, a sloping lawn spread out in front of them.

"Grandma, Charli and I are going to the paddocks to see a new horse who arrived this morning," said Jared. "Would you like to come with

44

us?"

"No. Off you go. I'd like to stay here and see what's happening."

"Sure you'll be okay?" asked Charli.

"I'll be fine. Let me know what you think of our new arrival."

"Will do," replied Jared as he and his sister walked toward the corral leaving Martha alone at the top of the hill. She scanned the site and a smile formed on her face. She loved the carnival atmosphere and the laughter of her patrons. The event had all the trademarks of being a success. Her heart swelled at the thought of her plans becoming a reality. Tears threatened to spill from her eyelids as she pictured the animals saved through their work on the ranch. She wiped them away. "Silly old fool," she muttered as she proceeded down the slope.

At the bottom of the hill, she could hear rows of vendors barking their wares. All sorts of products for pets, displayed in brightly colored booths, were available for the animal-loving public. To the left of the booths, a fenced off area was set up as a lure course for dogs. The group watched as a man and his dog entered the arena. On a signal, a fake squirrel attached to a monorail set out and zipped around the course. The dog, released from its lead, raced after the squirrel. After completing the circuit, the dog came back to her owner for a treat. People watching clapped as another dog waited at the start line. Crowds gathered to watch the antics of the animals. There were cheers for the racers and laughter for those who were either not interested in the chase and lay down, or those who decided to investigate interesting scents in a different part of the run. Martha watched for a while, then turned her attention to the barns and the renovated vet clinic on her right. Proud of the innovative facilities, she entered the office. She wandered around listening to the comments from visitors. A few who knew who she was complimented her on the ranch and the gleaming accommodations. She strolled through the door between the clinic and the barn, heading for Amazing Grace's stall. She was glad to see it was empty. One of the workers must have taken Grace and her foal out to the far pasture with the other horses where they wouldn't be disturbed by any of the crowd. Everything was in order in the barn, so she exited by the side door. She hadn't gone but a few steps when a voice hailed her.

"Mrs. Bancroft."

Her body rigid, she turned with a frown to the speaker. "Mr. Carter."

Montgomery Carter and his associate Harry Bales of Fern Glen Developments stood ten feet in front of her. She crossed her arms, waiting for him to speak.

"I couldn't miss the opportunity to see what you are planning for this property. It's interesting, but as you know, I think it could be better utilized by building a new enclave of homes for people. Now I know what you have in mind, I could reserve a portion of the area for a park for the children to play and even an off-leash park for their animals. What do you say? It would make you a lot of money and provide much needed homes for the people who wish to move to the Durham Region."

Martha drew herself up, threw her shoulders back and lifting her chin stared at her adversary in the regalest of poses. Eyes blazing fire, she spoke. "Mr. Carter. We've been over this many times before. I have absolutely no interest in selling this estate to you or any other developer. We are far too close to the Oak Ridges Moraine, and it would be foolish to build here, even if you could bribe your way into getting the permits needed. As long as I'm alive, we will not be selling. Enjoy your visit, but if this were the only reason you came, I would suggest you leave as soon as possible." Martha turned on her heel and strode off towards the house, fury emanating from every pore.

Chapter Thirteen

T he scene reverted to the living room where Mac was finishing his interview with Andrew.

"No wonder you want to save the ranch from the developers. What a horrid man," exclaimed Gladys.

"See. I told you. What are these two talking about now?"

"Let's listen."

"What did you do after dinner?" Mac asked.

Drew answered, "We all went our separate ways. Mother wished to meet at nine, but we were free until then."

"Where did you go?"

"I went to our room. I wanted to go over a dossier I had prepared for Tom. I have some exciting new plans for the ranch. I talked to him before dinner, but I wanted to go over them in more detail after the meeting. When it was close to nine, I put the papers in my satchel and headed to the library."

"You saw no one else?"

"No."

"About the meeting. Mr. Winslow mentioned it was to discuss your mother's plan for the estate and a new will."

"Yes."

Martha turned to Gladys. "Oh, you've gotta see the meeting. What a fiasco."

"Sure. Let's try this again." Once more the pair were observers to what happened earlier in the evening.

At nine o'clock on the dot, the family entered the library.

"Thank goodness that mangy mutt isn't around. He's a menace. Did you notice he almost bit me when I was saying hello to Grandmother?" Percy muttered to Adele.

"What did you say, Percy?" remarked Martha.

"I was wondering where our Zeus is, Grandmother."

Martha curled her lip. "'Our' Zeus is in our room." Looking at the rest of the group, she pointed to the chairs set in front of the desk.

"Please take a seat and I'll get right to the point."

"Oh goody, is this where we get our money, Andy?"

"Shut up, Vanessa," Andrew hissed.

Vanessa's head snapped back as if she'd been hit. She lowered her eyes and stumbled into one of the chairs.

Martha frowned at her son. Turning her attention back to the group, she continued. "As you know, your father and I bought this estate because we wanted to raise horses. Nothing huge, but a cause we could put our hearts into. Over the years we invested in the estate. We built the barns and bought breeding stock with a modicum of success.

"Hear, hear," shouted Andrew. "You've done a marvelous job, Mother. Our thoroughbreds have become renowned in the horse world. They put the Bancroft name on the racing map which, in turn, has given us valuable contacts for the business."

Martha looked at her son, a tiny smile lifting the corners of her mouth. "I'm glad you approve, Drew, as I've decided to expand a little. I have several areas of concern but want to focus on one. Rescuing horses. Since the Ontario Government's change of the rules at the racetracks, a lot of fine thoroughbreds are being auctioned off for slaughter. Every year more than 50,000 horses are killed for meat in Canada. I cannot hope to save them all but can rescue a few. I applied for and received approval three days ago to turn Bancroft Stables into a sanctuary for horses and, perhaps, dogs. Considering the go-ahead, I'm changing the name of Bancroft Stables to the Oak Ridges Oasis to better identify the purpose of the property. I'll probably call it the double O," she laughed.

"What?" shouted Andrew, springing from his chair.

"Sit down Drew. I've allocated funds for the redesign of the buildings on the property from my own private reserves and modified my will. I wanted you to hear the distribution from me in person. I want no misunderstanding. To achieve my goals, I have set up the Martha Bancroft Foundation which will be responsible for the care and upkeep of the animals and the sanctuary. I have deposited a sum from my current capital to start the fund. All money left at the time of my death will be added to it. A Board of Directors will be approved in the next couple of weeks. I asked Tom to be here tonight. He will confirm what I'm saying should any of you decide to challenge me in court. I've watched you for years and to say I am disappointed would be an understatement.

"Adele, since you're Ed's widow, you will be provided for, as you are now, from his estate. I will give you an additional $200,000 for your and Percy's use, but no more. These funds will be transferred to your account next week. In future, you will have to make do with what Ed left you. If you don't find the amount adequate for your needs, I suggest you go back to your secretarial career. The same goes for you, Percy. You need to find a viable job. Nothing else will be provided."

Adele gasped. She pulled her handkerchief from the wrist band of her dress and began to flutter it in front of her face. "Mother Bancroft! You can't mean it. You know I'm frail. I can't possibly work. As for Percy, he has delicate sensibilities and needs to pursue his artistic talents. It would never do for him to obtain a job and must associate with people of a lower class. It would crush him. No, no, what you're suggesting will not do for either of us."

"As you wish, Adele, but there will be no more funds forthcoming. If either of you wish to pursue a career, I will more than happily pay for your schooling and start up, but there will be nothing else."

Adele sank back into her chair, her face flushed, and her eyes closed.

Percy stood and put his hands on his mother's shoulders. "But, Grandmother, Mother is correct. I told you at dinner I'm in the middle of an exciting program with my music. You know we're going to Austria in a few weeks. You can't cut us off now. How will I get there?"

"Percy, I've investigated your program and it's an expensive fraud. The Maestro, as you call him, is a long-time con artist with no standing at all in the musical community. If you'd any real talent and were pursuing a career at a bona fide school of music, I'd encourage you, but this is a waste of time and money. I cannot support it. If you are determined to go, you will have to use part of the $200,000, but remember, there won't be any additional funds. Oh, get your mother's smelling salts. The two of you are quite impossible."

"You've been checking up on the Maestro?" stuttered Percy.

"Of course. I like to know where my money's going."

"Your money? It should have been my father's money. Then it should have come to me."

Martha's eyes narrowed and her body went rigid. She glared at her grandson, and every syllable laced with fury, she answered, "The money is your grandfather's and mine. Since we earned it, we get to say how it is spent. If you want more, earn it yourself."

Adele picked up her hankie and dabbed her eyes. She patted Percy's hand on her shoulder. "Oh, how could you say such horrid things? My heart is beating quite fast. Percy, please help me up. There's a dear boy. I'm going to our room to lie down."

Percy helped his mother to stand and escorted her from the room, his cheeks red and his mouth drawn in a tight line.

Martha turned to her son and said, "Now, Drew. Your turn. I have been distressed with some of your choices. You have squandered the inheritance from your father by living beyond your means and making foolish investments. But, since you are my only son, the sum of $500,000 will be transferred to your account to use as you wish. Your salary from the company will be increased slightly. If you want more capital, you'll have to grow the company, diversify, or sell it and start anew. It's what your father would have done. There is nothing else provided in my will."

Andrew's face mottled purple and eyes blazing, he sprang from his chair. "What? Outrageous. Mother, you can't be serious. You're abandoning me for an airy-fairy scheme? I've heard you talk about these plans of yours, but I didn't think you were serious!"

"When have I ever not been serious about plans for the estate?"

"Well, never, but this is preposterous! I couldn't believe you meant it. I have expenses to meet and obligations to uphold. I must retain my place in society and that takes money. I do have plans for the company and the estate in the works. I've been thinking of splitting the property into several sections. Of course, I will keep the house and the largest piece for you and the family, but we could make a pretty penny if we sold to the right developers. I have been meaning to talk to you about it for several months, but I wanted to wait until I had investors ready to move on a good deal. Everything is all lined up and with your go ahead, we can start negotiations immediately. It's time to get into the Asian market. We need to raise capital to expand operations. This is the perfect opportunity."

"Oh, but I do understand what you want to do. I've known for a while about your 'negotiations' with the Fern Glen Group. This property will not be sold to any developers. This land borders the Oak Ridges Moraine and there is no way I want it developed. Do you realize we lose a soccer field of farmland every second while adding two more people to the world population? We need all the good farmland we can get. The forest is now part of the Land Conservancy. It will never be developed. Also, we are losing our bees at an alarming rate. Do you know they need to take the nectar from two million flowers just to make one pound of honey? I will be planting wildflowers on the lower forty to assist them. As we progress, the house will be renovated to include a research/learning center for any help we can give to aid the planet. By the way, James Sinclair dropped by the other day. You remember him?

51

Chairman of the Board of Gateway? He mentioned the Board is quite alarmed about your expansion plans for the company. He emphasized how reckless and inadvisable they are in the current economic climate. I have made sure they will never happen."

Drew protested, "James and those other dinosaurs on the Board have no vision. They're locked into the last century and wouldn't agree to trying to grow the company even if my father proposed it."

"Your father had profound respect for James, as do I. There'll be no Asian expansion now. Come up with a new plan to advance our market share."

"You will not steal what is rightfully mine! We aren't farmers. We are Bancroft's. This lovely land wasted on a few mangy animals and crops to save bees, for God's sake. You've gone senile in your old age and been bamboozled by pseudo-scientific mumbo jumbo. I should have you declared incompetent!"

Vanessa exploded out of her chair. "You stupid jerk. How dare you talk to Mother like that. She can do what she wants. It's her property." Vanessa's body was shaking; she lifted her hand to her mouth. Glaring at her husband, she turned and fled the room.

"This isn't over, Mother. I will fight you in court. It's my money and I intend to get it. Nessa! Vanessa, wait." Andrew ran out of the room and down the hallway. The sound of the front door slamming echoed throughout the house. Then all was silent.

Martha slumped back in her chair and closed her eyes. "Well, that went about as well as I expected, although Vanessa was a surprise. I've never seen her stand up to him before. Wait 'til he learns Jared's in charge of the research facility and Charli will be working with you. You'd better prepare yourself for more fireworks. Tom, you, and I will discuss all the final details tomorrow. Jared, I got the blueprints from the contractors for the new barn. I think you'll be happy with their concept. I expect to move on this right away. Now, I'm going to bed. Oh, give me the papers for signing, Tom. I want to go over them before I see you in the morning."

"Are you sure I shouldn't hang on to them? I wouldn't want them to get lost."

"They'll be safe with me. You're behaving oddly this evening. What's up?"

"Nothing. It's just I know how important these transactions are for you and want to make sure everything goes as smoothly as possible. Here you go." Tom handed her a manila envelope containing the will and all the papers pertinent to the property changes. Clutching it under her arm, she got up and made her way out of the room. Ascending the stairs, she paused for a moment to catch her breath. A little steadier, she walked to her room, entered, and closed the door. She placed the envelope on her nightstand. After her nightly ritual, she picked up Zeus and put him on the bed. Climbing in, she turned on the lamp and reached for the pouch. Opening it, she withdrew the documents.

"So tired," she whispered to herself, dropping the papers on the covers beside her right hand. Zeus cuddled into her left side and laid his head on her lap. Exhaling a big sigh, she stroked his soft fur. Closing her eyes, she leaned back into the pillows. Should she sign the new will or leave the old one in place? She thought about her plans and all the good they could do. But, was she being fair to her family?

Chapter Fourteen

The image faded and Martha and Gladys were back in the sitting room where Mac was finishing with Andrew.

"How did you feel about the changes she was going to make?"

"They were absurd! I was never so humiliated in my life. She was going to leave this estate as a shelter for God only knows what wretched beasts, the surrounding estate to a forest conservancy, and the house as a research facility. I was to be given $500,000, a raise in pay and the monthly stipend I get from my father's estate. She must have been crazy. How am I supposed to maintain the family's standing in this community on such a paltry sum?"

"What did you do?"

"I told Mother the plans for the property were outrageous. I said I'd put a stop to it. For some reason, Vanessa got upset with me and ran out of the room. After I told Mother I would be consulting my lawyers, I ran after Vanessa, and we drove around for a while."

"Never could see farther than the wart on his nose. Foolish man," whispered Martha. She bobbed around Gladys in agitation.

"Keep still. You're getting agitated again and starting to flash. Keep it up and they'll see you."

"Did you see the new will," asked Mac.

"At the meeting."

"But not since you left?"

"No."

"As far as you know it hasn't been signed?"

"That's right. Why? Do you know something we don't?"

"Who inherits under the old will?"

"Adele and I do. The house and the estate are split between the two of us, as well as a part of my mother's capital. After disbursements to our ranch employees, and a substantial benefit to my son Jared, my daughter Charlotte and my nephew, Percy, the rest of the estate goes to us."

"What time did you arrive back at the house?"

"I dunno. We drove around for a while talking about things. Must have been eleven-thirty... maybe nearer twelve."

"What did you do after returning?"

"Went to my room and prepared for bed."

"And your wife?"

"I don't know where she went but was told this morning she took a hot toddy to my mother. I was asleep by the time she came to bed."

"Thank you, Mr. Bancroft. We're finished here. Please ask your wife to come in."

Andrew stood. "If the will turns up, let me know. There's no time to be wasted if I want to make a claim against it." He left the room as Mac continued to write in his notebook. Hearing the door open again, he looked up to see Vanessa entering the room.

"Mrs. Bancroft. Please take a seat."

"Didn't Andy tell you everything?"

"Yes, but I'd like to hear what you have to say." Mac led her through their arrival and the events which resulted in them leaving and returning to the house. "What time did you arrive back at the house?"

"I guess it was around midnight."

"What did you do?"

"Well, Andy went up to our room, but I was still angry. I was going to go into the library, but I could see a light on and thought someone might be in there and I didn't want to talk to anybody."

"Do you know who was in the library?"

"No."

"What did you do?"

"I went upstairs and saw Mother Bancroft's light was still on. I hoped she wasn't awake worrying about Andy. Then I thought, 'I know. I'll make her hot toddy'. She loves her hot toddies. In fact, it's quite a joke in the family. I thought it might help her sleep. I went downstairs to the kitchen and made one. You should let it sit for five minutes while the spices, lemon and whiskey mingle to get the best flavour. I put the mug down on the table and went into the pantry because I thought I heard a noise. I couldn't find anything, but I'm sure it was a mouse. I don't really like them, so I'm glad I didn't see one," she said shivering.

"You left the mug on the table while you went into the pantry?"

"Yes."

"Does anyone else in the family drink toddies?"

"No. The men think all the spices ruin good whiskey and Adele and I prefer hot chocolate."

"If a member of the family saw the mug on the table, they would presume it would be for Mrs. Bancroft? They wouldn't pick it up and drink it themselves?"

"Oh, no. Only Mother drank them. No one else would touch it."

"What did you do then?"

"I went upstairs to take her the toddy."

"Was she awake?"

"Yes, and she thanked me very much. I told her things would be better in the morning and I hoped she had a good night's sleep. Then I kissed her and left the room."

"Nothing else happened?"

"No," said Vanessa, her eyes looking at the floor.

"You're sure. You seem a little hesitant."

"I'm sure," she replied lifting her chin and looking Mac in the eye.

Mac stared back at her, but Vanessa stared him down until finally he put down his pen. "Thank you, Mrs. Bancroft. That will be all for now."

He picked up his pen and wrote in his notebook. Vanessa stood, a frown wrinkling her brow. She turned and left the room.

"Vanessa. Come back. Tell him about the will," shouted Martha. Her energy was pulsating fast, pushing out into the room. The lights flickered and the audio player started to play the finale of Tchaikovsky's 1812 overture.

"Calm down. She can't hear you," shouted Gladys. "Now look what you've done."

"Hot damn," exclaimed Martha in astonishment. "This being energy is neat. What else can I do?"

"Lots of things, but you need to turn it off. Look at Mac."

Martha looked. At the first blare of sound, Mac threw his pen up into the air and jumped from his seat. Hands over his ears, he ran to the console and looked for the off switch. Joe slammed open the door and rushed in.

"Holy crap! What the hell is that?"

"Dunno. Damn thing started playing out of nowhere. Almost shit my pants!"

The two men checked all over the machine, but there didn't appear to be an on/off switch.

"Oops. It's hooked up to a switch in the wall. It was the last thing I played before the family arrived yesterday. Needed to blow off some steam and the cannons and bells work for me. How do I turn it off?"

Gladys brightened her energy a little and silence fell like a drop cloth on the room. "There. You'll get the hang of things but be careful. Energy doesn't discriminate and you can cause a lot of damage until you get used to it."

"Hmm. This could come in handy. Wonder if he senses I'm here?"

Ears ringing, Mac walked back to the table. "Give me five minutes, Joe. Then bring in Mrs. Adele Bancroft."

"Will do." Joe left the room and closed the door.

Mac sat at the desk for a minute staring around the room. "I need air."

Chapter Fifteen

Mac got up from his chair and stepped out the French doors. On the surface, this looked like a case of an elderly lady dying in her sleep, but he wasn't satisfied. Andrew Bancroft was a bit shifty, and Mac was sure Vanessa was hiding something. He looked at his watch and frowned. He'd hoped to get home in time for breakfast, but at the rate they were going, it wasn't likely. He was not looking forward to the next interview. Walking back into the room, he walked over to the door and spoke to Joe. A few minutes later, Adele entered the room. Mac got up and held the chair for her.

"This should be good," whispered Martha.

"Please take a seat, Mrs. Bancroft. I have a few questions to ask about your visit here last evening. I'll try to take as little time as possible."

Before he could begin, the door opened again, and Percy sauntered in the room.

"Percy Bancroft. My mother has a heart condition, and I don't want her upset any more than necessary. I will be sitting in on the interview, if you don't mind, dear boy."

Mac raised his one eyebrow and looked down at his notebook.

"That's fine, Mr. Bancroft. Joe, bring Mr. Bancroft a chair."

Joe soon returned with a chair for Percy. He sashayed to the chair, sat down, and crossed his legs. Flipping his scarf behind him, he took his mother's hand and patted it. Mac took his position and got out his pen.

"Now, Mrs. Bancroft. I understand you and Percy arrived together?"

"Oh, yes. It's a long drive from the city and Percy was kind enough to pick me up and drive me here."

"What happened when you arrived?"

"Well, let me see. Mother Bancroft….," she broke off crying into her handkerchief. "Oh, I will never get used to her being gone. She was such a lovely woman. An outstanding citizen and philanthropist. I…"

"You were saying?" Mac interrupted.

"Yes, well, they were all in the living room," barked Adele.

"All?"

"Mother Bancroft, Thomas, Andrew and Vanessa."

"Dr. Jared Bancroft had not yet arrived?"

"The golden boy? No. He is always fashionably, or otherwise, late."

"Where were you Mr. Bancroft when your mother entered the living room?"

"I took our cases up to our rooms. Then I joined the group for a pre-dinner sherry, while we waited for my cousin."

"Does everyone stay in the same rooms when they come?"

"Yes."

"Can you give me the layout of the rooms upstairs?"

"The family quarters are to the left of the main staircase. As you go up the stairs the first door on your right is usually Thomas's room. Then the next room on your right is where Andrew and Vanessa stay. Across the hall from Thomas is my room and my mother's next to it. There is a connecting door between the two rooms so I can reach Mother, if she requires assistance during the night. Grandmother's room is at the end of the hall. It is the largest bedroom and overlooks the fields of the ranch. The rooms are small suites containing a bathroom and a reading area in each. To the right of the staircase are similar rooms for any other guests, such as my Aunt Ruth, cousins Jared or Charlotte. Aunt Ruth was not invited for dinner or the meeting afterwards."

"Any particular reason?"

"Well, it would not be done, dear boy. Rather gauche if you ask me. Ruth is Andrew's first wife, and it would be a bit awkward to say the least."

"But they have rooms in the house. I presume they were on good terms with your grandmother?"

"Yes. They were on excellent terms. She never did approve of the divorce. Also, Jared is the vet for the ranch and Charlotte assists him in his work. I take it there was an emergency this weekend, so they were staying here, although Charlotte didn't attend dinner or the reading of the will. My Aunt Ruth was not here."

"Mrs. Vanessa Bancroft is Andrew's second wife? How was she received by the rest of the family?"

"Everyone thought she was a gold-digging tart."

"Besides being incredibly stupid," sniffed Adele.

"Any reason for the judgment?"

"It wasn't a judgment! I'm simply stating the facts. Her mother was a laundress or house cleaner or some such thing. Widowed after the war and they lived down in a poorer section of town. Vanessa worked as a waitress at the racetrack, for goodness sake. She certainly moved a step up the ladder by snagging Andrew. They had an affair, you know, before he divorced Ruth. Mother was not at all pleased by that, let me tell you. She tried to put a stop to it, but he ended up running off to Vegas with her shortly after his divorce was final. Shocked everyone. Disgraceful conduct. I whole heartedly agreed with Mother."

"I understand you all went into dinner once Dr. Bancroft arrived."

"Yes."

"How was dinner?"

"Well, if you ask me, the meat was a little dry and I'm sure Mother Bancroft could have chosen a better wine, but all in all, it wasn't too bad."

"I don't think that's what he's asking, Mother. Do you mean 'how did everyone act?'"

"Yes, Mr. Bancroft."

Percy continued. "They were all a bit snippy. Mother explained how she had found a wonderful new doctor who was going to do several tests. We are optimistic he'll make Mother right as rain, don't we? But

60

do you think any of them cared. Not one bit. Then I told them about my trip to Europe with the Maestro. I thought at least they would be happy for me! But no. Peasants. All they could do was to cast aspersions on his genius and mock me. Disgusting, the lot of them."

"I understand after dinner you had some free time until the meeting at nine. What did you do?"

"After our ordeal at supper, I retired to my room with a migraine. Percy walked me to the room, gave me my medication and closed the curtains so I could lie down in comfort."

"And what did you do Mr. Bancroft?"

"I went to my own room to work on my music for the Maestro."

"You saw no one?"

"No."

"Then at nine you went to the library?"

"Yes."

"How did the meeting go?"

"Not well. My Grandmother had a crazy notion of saving wildlife. Can you believe it? As if we were farmers. Apparently, it has been in the works for a while, but I'd never heard of it before last night. Had you, Mother?"

"No. I never heard of it before."

"Anyway. The whole thing is ridiculous."

"How so?"

"This ranch has been in our family for years and has built up quite a reputation as a top-drawer breeding stable. What on earth would make her want to turn it into a sanctuary for flea-bitten nags and then to want to plant this lovely acreage with grain or whatever she was planning to do? Why, it's atrocious. And the house. Turn this lovely home into a research facility? We'd be the laughingstock of Durham. Thank God she hadn't signed the will."

"How do you know it wasn't signed? Did you see it?"

"Well, no, but she talked about signing it later, so I presume it

61

wasn't signed."

"Did she provide adequately for the family?"

"Hardly. A mere pittance. She had the gall to suggest Mother and I get jobs. A job! Can you imagine? I was mortified and Mother nearly had a stroke. I had to escort her to her room and calm her down."

"Did you see what happened to the will after the meeting ended?"

"No. I presume Thomas has it."

"What did you do then, Mr. Bancroft?"

"Me? Ummm… I went out to the barns to cool down. I needed to think about how to approach Grandmother in the morning. I came back in and went into the library when I heard that stupid mutt howling. Then we all ran to Grandmother's room."

"And you, Mrs. Bancroft. Did you stay in your room?

"Well, no. After Percy left, I went back to the library. I needed a drink to calm my nerves and since everyone had left, I thought I would get privacy there."

"And did you?"

"For a while. Then Jared came in and we talked. Then Percy arrived. We were chatting when we heard the dog howl, so we naturally ran to find out what was wrong."

"Thank you for your time. If I have any further questions, I'll be in touch."

Percy helped his mother to her feet and assisted her out of the room, closing the door behind them.

Chapter Sixteen

M ac called Joe into the room. He took the seat opposite Mac. Martha and Gladys watched and listened from their corner.

"Sheesh, what a family. Doesn't look like anyone is going to miss the old lady. Not sure there's enough for a motive for murder, though. Wish I could find the will. Nobody knows where it is, or so they claim. One thing I did learn, Vanessa Bancroft was the one who made the hot toddy and took it to her mother-in-law. She did leave it sitting unattended for at least five minutes. Be enough time for a person to come in and tamper with it. I imagine the cloves, cinnamon and nutmeg would mask the odor and flavor of the toxin if there was one. If poison was involved, no one had an alibi for the time in question."

"Poison? That can't be right. Murdered?" gasped Martha. "By my own family. I know they were angry, but murder? Why would they want to kill me?"

"Why not? You were about to make some substantial changes to their inheritance. Greed brings out the worst in people."

"You're leaning towards murder rather than natural causes?" asked Joe.

"We'll have to wait for the results of the autopsy, but I wouldn't put it past this lot."

"Anyone in particular stand out?"

"Hell, it could be any of them. Well, I better get back to it. Bring in Mr. Jared Bancroft, Joe."

"Sure thing, Mac."

Joe got up and called Jared into the room. He took a seat as Joe left and closed the door.

"I'm sorry for your loss, Dr. Bancroft."

"Thank you. I'm really going to miss her."

"I understand you are the vet for the estate. Correct?"

"Yes. Both Charli and I work with the animals. Charli assists me and she also produces the salves, lotions, and other products we sell."

"Charli is your sister, Charlotte Bancroft?"

"Yes."

"And how does your father feel about the two of you working here?"

"Father loves to schmooze with the high and mighty. Fancies himself as a future Prime Minister. Having his offspring mucking around in horse shit isn't his idea of the "ideal" family. Not enough prestige."

"Can you tell me about your visit here last evening?"

"Grandma summoned us last week for dinner tonight. She was quite a gal. Imperious, but kind and loving to those less fortunate. And smart. You couldn't put much over on her."

"See, I told you I wasn't all bad," muttered Martha.

"Never said you were," answered Gladys. The two turned their attention back to the interview.

"I understand there was a new will in play. Do you know if your grandmother signed it?"

"No. She took it with her last night, and I haven't seen it since."

"And if the new one isn't found signed, the old one is in effect. How would you feel if that happens?"

"Sad. If my dad gets his hands on the estate, what remains will be sold to developers. He may even try to revoke the conservancy."

"You're concerned... why?"

"This property is close to the Oak Ridges Moraine. It will be shoving the envelope a little further, trying to build on the Moraine. That can never be allowed. It would destroy all the headwaters downstream. Our water supply would never recover."

"Atta boy, you tell him," chortled Martha.

"Shh."

"It seems like there's rift between you and your father."

64

"Unfortunately, yes. He cares more about the money and business than he ever did about his family."

"I understand Mrs. Vanessa Bancroft is his second wife. How do you feel about her?"

"Oh, Vanessa's not so bad. She's only two years older than me. Dad needed some arm candy and she fit the bill. She's not the sharpest pencil in the box which suits him fine. He treats her like garbage. I'm surprised she hasn't left him, but she gets to live in a nice house and indulge in her favorite pastime – shopping. All she has to do is look pretty and be there when he wants her. It's a perfect setup for both."

"What about your aunt and cousin? How did they feel about the new will?"

"Aunt Adele and Percy? They hated it. Grandma was going to cut them off with a two hundred thousand payout and nothing more. They are the most irritating people on the planet. Grandma could always put them in their place. She was a master of sarcasm. She could slice you up one side and down the other without you feeling the blade cut. I loved to watch her when she got a full head of steam."

"You were never subject to her wit?"

"Oh, I had my fair share growing up, but I deserved it. She and I got along because we understood each other. We both knew there were more important things to life than bridge, theater, social standing, and the lot. The others didn't understand her at all. They thought she was a cantankerous old lady who should be put out to pasture."

Mac put down his pen and notebook. "Thank you, Dr. Bancroft. That is all for now. We may have further questions. Please, don't go anywhere without letting the Department know where you will be."

Chapter Seventeen

After Jared left, Mac sat at the small table writing in his notebook. Joe entered the room and sat in the chair Jared had vacated.

"Learn anything new?"

"Nope. Colorful cast of characters. Where'd they go after they left here?"

"Andrew went down the hall to the other side of the house. Been told there's a well-stocked library down there. Mrs. Vanessa Bancroft went toward the kitchen. Percy went out the front door. Said he 'needed some clean air after his interrogation'. His mother went toward the library. Dr. Bancroft said he was going to the barn."

"Dr. Walsh is waiting for me. I'd better talk to her. What time you got?"

"My watch says five-thirty."

"Great. I'll finish with the doc, and we can be on our way. At least we should be able to find a good breakfast."

"Sounds good. I'll write up my notes and wait for you in the car. Too bad about the old lady. Seems like she had great plans for this place."

"Yeah, well if my suspicions are correct, someone didn't want her to complete them."

"Let's go to the kitchen," said Martha. "I want to hear what Mac has to say to the coroner." The two spirits vanished.

The men got up from their chairs and left the room. Joe stayed in the empty living room to complete his notes and Mac walked down the hall which led to the rear of the house. Martha and Gladys watched from their perch at the top of the multi-paned window which looked over the hills and barns dotting the property. They dimmed their light as much as they could, hoping to blend in with the moonlight. Mac saw them as soon as he entered the kitchen, a frown creasing his brow.

"Uh-oh. He's spotted us. Stay as still as you can," whispered Gladys.

He continued to stare at them for a minute, but as they didn't move, he shrugged his shoulders and looked around. To his left, he saw an oversized pantry with rows of shelving bearing an extensive quantity of jars of preserves, tubs of lard, canned goods, sacks of flour, and dry goods. Beside the pantry wall, a door led to the outside. Mac scanned the distance from the table to the door. Could a person come in, doctor a drink, and leave without Vanessa seeing or hearing them? He'd do a test with Joe later. In the centre of the room sat a thick wooden table with twelve chairs gathered around. Loads of cupboards and counter space, plus a state-of-the-art industrial stove and fridge said here was the heart of the ranch. Cissy sat at the kitchen table working on her laptop. She looked up as Mac joined her.

"All done?"

"Yeah. Finished with the lot of them. Sorry to have kept you, but since I had you here, I wanted to let you know how much I've enjoyed working with you in the past. You seem to see things differently than most people and I'd like to work with you on this one, providing it is a case. I've heard of old lady Bancroft around town and most people liked her and agreed with what she was trying to accomplish here. Tough old broad, though. Some of the stories I've heard, would make milk curdle," he grinned.

"Really?"

"Let's just say you didn't want to get on her wrong side. Her sarcastic wit could leave you quaking in your shoes. She's left more than one bureaucrat cut to shreds if he dared oppose what she wanted done. That said, she had a reputation for being fair and generous. I'm hoping this is natural death, but if it's not, damned if I want someone to get away with stopping her."

"I understand. Well, glad to have your help, Mac. I can make the

67

request if you want."

"Thanks, Doc. I appreciate it."

"My friends call me Cissy. Why don't you?" smiled Cissy.

"Cissy, it is."

Martha chuckled. "I can see a budding romance. Be a nice outcome of this sordid mess. Let's follow them out to her car."

"Don't be nosy. Maybe he wants private time with her," Gladys retorted.

"I'm not being nosy. I'm investigating my death. Besides, I love a good romance. We can move it along."

"We don't have time for such sentiments. We need to get home."

"Lighten up. We'll get there. I'm having a little fun while we wait."

Martha vanished. With a sigh, Gladys did the same.

Mac looked up at the window as he escorted Cissy from the room. The lights were gone. A small fissure of shock tickled his nape. "Did you see the lights at the top of the window?" he asked.

"No. Why?"

"I don't know. It was weird. When I came to get you, there were two lights up at the top corner of the window. It was odd because they couldn't be a reflection. There's nothing there to reflect. Now they're gone. This house is getting to me. I need breakfast."

Cissy laughed. "Could be Martha."

"A ghost? Don't exist."

"You're sure?"

"Yes."

"Glad you're so positive. I'll have to tell you about my experiences."

"Love to hear your stories, but once you're dead, you're dead. That's it."

Cissy's laugh echoed as they stepped out into a beautiful night, with stars twinkling overhead.

"Lovely night after all the rain. Going to be a good day."

They walked down to where Cissy was parked in the deep gloom near the entrance to the ranch. "Hot damn! Those are some badass wheels," exclaimed Mac.

"Down, big boy," laughed Cissy. "Never seen a truck before?"

Mac circled the truck, touching it with reverent strokes. "Sure, but this is a real beauty. Not a choice I expected a woman like you to drive."

"'A woman like me'… hmmm… meaning?"

"Ummm, sorry, that came out wrong. I meant you're a professional woman and… shit, I'm digging myself in deeper."

Cissy laughed. "You'd better quit while you're ahead. I do a lot of off-road exploring, going on outdoor retreats and stuff. I find it great for toting my tent, gear, firewood, tools, and anything else I might need. I have a small car for work, but I was out when the Sergeant called. Came straight here. Didn't have time to go home and switch rides."

"You camp as well as own a truck? Be still my heart. Will you marry me?"

"Later Alligator. I've got a party to go to this weekend and an autopsy to do on Monday, so my plate's rather full now."

Martha and Gladys were hiding in the shrubs near the car listening to the banter.

"Ya know, the energy here is dense and dark," whispered Gladys. "Something's out of whack. I don't like it."

"I feel it too," replied Martha.

"We need to follow her when she leaves."

"Okay by me," replied Martha.

Cissy opened the truck door and climbed into the driver's seat. She started the ignition and rolled down the window.

"Night Mac. We'll talk later."

"Night Cissy. You have my cell. Call if you need anything and don't forget, first free weekend, we're getting married!"

Cissy laughed and blew him a kiss. She watched as he turned and walked back to the house. Not hard to look at. Not at all. After one last look, she turned the car around and drove out the gates, the spirit guardians following in her wake.

Chapter Eighteen

Turning north, Cissy tuned the radio to a soothing channel so she could think about what just happened. Mac had asked her to join forces on this case if there was one. Thinking about working with him again gave her happy little shivers of delight. *Don't go there. Keep your mind on the case.* She turned her thoughts to the cadaver and what results she might find from the autopsy. It always amazed her how each body was different and yet the same. In her career, she had made fascinating discoveries. Every time she worked on a corpse; she was traveling to a different yet familiar country.

As she left the estate, fog shrouded the road. Long tendrils of ghostly fingers wafted in front of her. Cissy gripped the steering wheel and slowed down. Squinting her eyes and focusing on the road ahead, she pressed the high beams to better illuminate the asphalt and the trees off to the side. The fog cleared as she got closer to the town line. She loosened her grip on the steering wheel and pressed the accelerator. Cresting a hill, she saw movement from the corner of her eye. From the woods, off to her left, a large racoon lumbered in front of the car. Cissy gasped, slammed on the brakes, and wrenched the steering wheel to avoid hitting the creature. Her foot went to the floorboard. She pumped the brakes trying to slow down as she descended the slope, but nothing slowed the speed of the vehicle.

"The brakes aren't working. She's losing control," shouted Martha. "What do we do?"

"Increase your energy and join with mine."

The two spirits joined and formed a gigantic force field which

71

looked like a spider web of lightning flashing blue. They slid under the truck to hold it aloft as it became airborne. Crackling and popping sounds, like someone was playing with a large piece of bubble wrap, echoed in the night. The truck crossed the intersection, flew over the ditch and fence, and floated down onto a field. The pickup shuddered and coughed to a standstill as the force field dissipated. All was silent.

"We did it," cried Martha.

"Whew. Could have been much worse," said Gladys. "I'm glad we followed her. Looks like somebody tampered with the brakes."

"Why would anyone hurt the doctor? Doesn't make sense."

"My guess is they're mad she called for an autopsy. Expected a simple death by natural causes. Threw them for a loop."

"Hmm... doesn't sound good for me. Maybe I was murdered after all."

Dazed, Cissy rested her head on the steering wheel gulping in deep breaths. She began her routine of long breath in, long breath out to relax her muscles and slow her heart rate. Once she had regained control, she raised her head and leaned back in the seat. What was the strange glow she saw before the car became airborne? And the sounds? Come to think of it, it was a soft landing for how fast she was going. She got out of her truck to look for any damage. Her legs wobbled as she tried to stand. As the strength came back into her body, she walked around the vehicle inspecting it for anything broken or bent. Everything was intact. The hairs on her nape prickled. Something protected her, but what or who? Martha? She grinned. Looking up to the sky, she said, "Martha, if you're there, thanks for the help."

Martha chortled. "I told you she was special. She knows there's more to life than what can be felt with human senses. She'll find out what happened to me."

When Cissy finished her inspection, she reached for her purse and pulled out her cell.

"Mac, it's Cissy."

"Hey Cissy. What's up?"

"I've had an accident."

"Where are you?"

"Up Ashburn at Chalk Lake Road."

"I'll be right there. You all right?"

"A little shaken is all."

"Do you need an ambulance?"

"No, but I will need a tow."

"No problem. Hang in there."

"And Mac... thanks."

"Hold on. We'll be there soon."

"Be careful. There's a few tricky fog patches on Ashburn."

Cissy sat in her truck and waited, thinking about what had happened. Fog was creeping in again and she shivered. Rubbing her hands up and down her arms, she kept watch in the rear-view mirror. After what seemed like an hour, but was probably closer to ten minutes, she spotted headlights coming up the road.

"Here they come," said Martha. "She'll be safe now. Let's go back to the house." The two spirits vanished from the scene.

Cissy stepped down. A car stopped, sending its high beams into the field. She heard the doors slam as Mac and Joe rushed to her side.

"What happened?"

"A racoon darted out in front of me. I slammed on the brakes, but the pedal went right to the floor. I don't understand. I had it in the shop three days ago for regular maintenance. They would have noticed if the brakes were faulty."

"I've called for a tow. We'll haul it back to the police compound and look. Meanwhile, let's get you to your friend's place. You said it's close to here?"

"Yeah. It's just up the road."

"Good."

Taking her arm, he led her back to the police car as Joe walked over to her truck to examine it.

"Climb in. Joe, I'm going to take the doc to her friend's house. Don't let the tow truck move the car until I'm back.'

"Sure, Mac."

Mac drove Cissy on to the house. As they approached the lane leading to her friend's house, he noticed an arched entranceway with the sign 'Thor's Sanctuary' written on it.

"This is your friend's place? I've driven by it several times."

"Yes. It belongs to David and Rebecca Connacher. Rebecca is my best friend. She and her husband have their landscaping business here. Its original name was Stone Cottage, but Becca changed it after a series of unusual circumstances. Along with their flower business, she runs a sanctuary for lost or unwanted dogs as well. It's a long story but quite fascinating. I'll have to get her to tell you."

"Unusual circumstances, eh? Do I want to know? Speaking of Thor, though, I've often wondered who he was."

"Ah. He was an incredibly special dog."

Reaching the end of the lane, Mac stopped the car, and they got out.

"Get some rest. I'll be back later tomorrow when I find out about your truck."

"Thanks, Mac. I appreciate your help."

Mac stared into Cissy eyes for a long moment. He reached up and brushed a stray lock of hair behind her ear. He started to lean into her but then abruptly turned on his heel and went back to his car. Climbing in, he gave her a final wave and drove down the lane.

Chapter Nineteen

F our hours later, Cissy stumbled into the kitchen at Stone Cottage and plunked down in a chair putting her head in her hands. "God, what a night. I feel like an elephant walking through molasses." She looked up, sniffing the air. "What is that wonderful smell?"

Rebecca turned from her stance at the stove and looked at her best friend. "Well, good morning to you Sunshine. Freshly baked bread and coffee which we will be enjoying in a bit. What time did you get in?"

"Mmmm. A little after six, I think. I've lost track of time. What time is it now?"

Rebecca poured a steaming cup of java and brought it to the table, setting it in front of Cissy. "Just after ten."

"Really? Ugh. No wonder I'm so tired." She lifted the mug and breathed in the aroma of the coffee. "Umm. Perfect. Thanks." She took a sip and settled back in her chair. "Martha Bancroft passed away during the night and Mac wants a full autopsy. I've scheduled it for Monday morning."

"Mac... as in the delicious hunk of male detective you sometimes work with? Interesting. Martha Bancroft? Is she the woman who lives in the huge ranch over near Ashburn?"

"She's the one. Appears to have died in her sleep. Or at least it's what the family is hoping. Mac isn't sure and we need to be sure. He asked if he could help me with the case if there is one. And yes, that's the Mac we're talking about."

"Ummm. Asked if he could assist in your investigation? Won't be too hard to work alongside of him, now will it?" laughed Rebecca.

"Becca, you can put your romance antenna back into your head. There's nothing going on between us."

"So you say. You've worked with him a few times over the last

75

couple of years, haven't you?"

"Yes, but we're only colleagues."

"Doesn't mean there couldn't be more. You're both single, attractive adults. Just sayin'."

"Right. Well, I'd better get dressed if I'm to help with this party."

"Ok, change the subject. I can take a hint. I'll fix you up a bite of breakfast," said Rebecca holding up her hands as Cissy was about to protest.

"When was the last time you ate?"

"I had a… ummm."

"That's what I thought. Scoot. Besides, it'll give us a little girl time before the hordes come in."

Cissy made her way up the stairs and into the shower. The warm water and citrus scented bath gel swept the cobwebs out of her head. By the time she finished drying her hair and dressing, she felt invigorated and revived. True to her promise, Becca had the coffee, oatmeal with fruit and toast prepared and on the table.

"Wow. Looks and smells delicious," said Cissy salivating as she took a seat.

Becca poured them both a mug and sat in the chair opposite her. As Cissy ate, Becca gazed around the room. A rush of gratitude and joy flooded her heart. She remembered the old mud room which had been here before it was renovated into a cozy kitchen. Framed in blue and white chintz curtains, a grand window, sparkling in the sunlight, graced the back wall, replacing the tiny, cracked windows which overlooked Becca's prized herb garden. Heated tiles in a mottled Country Blue replaced the old wood flooring, warming her toes on a wintry morning. A sturdy oak table with chairs sat in a small bay window alcove on the side wall allowing the room to flood with light and displaying a vista of woodlands and flowers as far as the eye could see. The table, covered in a blue chintz tablecloth which matched the curtains, held a white vase in which a fragrant mixture of white daisies, white baby's breath and small blue irises were arranged in a lovely bouquet.

"Woo hoo... earth to Becca."

"What? Oh. Sorry. I was thinking about this kitchen and all the changes we've made. Can you believe it's been three years? And yet, it seems like I've always been here."

"The kitchen's beautiful," said Cissy. She leaned over and took Becca's hand. "I'm happy to see you well again. You seem to be thriving working with David. Don't miss Wainwright Industries?"

"Not one bit. James is doing a fantastic job. He's hired a couple of top-notch execs and has been able to finally put his own stamp on the company. He's happy and I'm delighted for him. Last year he and Kat took a cruise to East Asia, and they are happier than ever. But, enough about me. What's going on in your world?"

"Same old, same old. Busy and with this new case, if it is a case, my time will be pretty filled up. The new house is great. I love Brooklin. I have great shopping in town and if I need big box stores, I'm only minutes away. Now the new 407 is through, I can zip to work in no time."

"But?"

"But I'm lonely. Ever since Kevin left six months ago, I've been feeling a little empty."

"He never deserved you anyway. Total tool!"

"True, but it wasn't all bad. We had some good times."

"Hah. Like the weekend in Niagara where you ran into his ex?"

"What a disaster!" laughed Cissy.

"Ya think?"

The two friends put down their coffee cups and looked at each other. Their eyes twinkled.

"You should've seen his face when she showed up at the door in a red peignoir holding a champagne bottle and two glasses," Cissy snickered.

"I'd rather have seen her face when she saw you in the suite."

"Yeah, it was pretty funny. Talk about mixed signals. Would've

77

made a great Neil Simon play."

The girls started to laugh and soon tears were rolling down their faces. Becca clutched her stomach while Cissy threw back her head and hooted. Pulling herself together, Cissy hiccupped. "I haven't laughed that much in ages. Oh, it's good to have my best friend back."

"It's good to be back," Becca said smiling. "And good riddance to Mr. Smarmy Pants. You'll find a guy who'll love you for you. I mean, what's not to love?"

"Right. I've told you about the reactions I get. A date scenario. 'And what do you do for a living?' 'Oh, I dissect dead bodies and examine them.' If King Willie was starting to rise to the occasion, it kinda deflates the mood, doncha think? Add to that, I'm not your typical 'little woman' with all my weird interests. What man's interested in a lady who gets excited by the discovery of ancient bones in the interior of a lost jungle rather than who won what in sports? I mean, my last real vacation was to Machu Picchu. And I got an invitation to a Neolithic dig in Scotland next summer." She rubbed her hands together. "An ancient settlement gets my blood stirring."

"So, you're a bit quirky, but you do clean up nicely. I happen to love quirky. I'm sure there's a fella who will love all your idiosyncrasies like I do. Maybe Mac?"

"Becca!"

"Alright. I'll stop. For now. Wow. Look at the time. We'd better get a move on if we want to get everything ready for the party. Can you believe the twins are thirteen? Me. With teenagers. Oh, Lord help us."

"Hey, my adopted nieces are great."

"Yeah, well you're not with them all the time. They're gonna be happy to see you. Party's at seven. I'm giving you the chore of putting up the decorations while I make the cake and see to the food. Mom's coming with James and Kat and their kids, along with David's sister and her companion with their three. It should be a full house."

"Your wish is my command, my lady," said Cissy standing and bowing to Becca. "Give me your sparklies and baubles, point me in the

78

right direction and I'll put up such a dazzling display even the top window dresser at Holt Renfrew will be put to shame."

Chapter Twenty

Decoration bags in hand, Cissy paused in the doorway to the living room. This was where Becca first encountered the ghost of Annie. Renovations had rendered it vastly different than it had been in Annie's time. A new hand-carved, burled oak mantle graced the old fieldstone fireplace, the *pièce de résistance* of the chamber. Pot lights twinkled from the ceiling. Gone was the old horsehair couch. In its place sat a chocolate brown leather reclining sofa, holding three overstuffed pillows in patterns of bright orange. The patina of an oak credenza sparkled in the sun's rays coming from the two front windows. Two stuffed occasional chairs flanked either side of the cabinet. A red chair from the old Maple Leaf Gardens sat along the wall to the left of the entranceway. It, and a large screen TV, which hung above the mantle, proclaimed David's love of all things sports. Since the Cubs had won the world's series in 2016, David's die-hard love for the Toronto Maple Leafs was rekindled into a bright flame. Maybe this would be the year they'd bring home the Stanley Cup! Cissy snorted at the thought.

"As if," she laughed.

Breaking free from her reverie, she moved into the room and placed the bags on the couch. She pulled the baubles and crepe paper from the sack and laughed when she saw them. The twins, Amy, and Bella, identical in looks were polar opposites when it came to style, attitude, and demeanor. To Bella, the entire world was hers to explore and conquer. She was fierce in her determination to see and do as much as she could in her lifetime. Full of inquisitive adventure, she flitted from one great cause to another relishing each new project with a curiosity and zeal which left others tired just watching her. Amy, on the other hand, was a solitary dreamer, who loved to cocoon in their tree house with her cat and books. Her adventures took place in her imagination, and she eagerly wrote story after story containing remarkable characters in fascinating worlds. The decorations reflected their personalities. Bright, bold colors for Bella; soft, dreamy pastels for Amy.

Cissy had been on the job for a couple of hours when Rebecca came into the room.

"Wow, looking fabulous, dahling. They're going to love it. I've just finished the cakes. See what you think."

Rebecca slipped her arm through Cissy's and the two friends made their way to the kitchen.

"I'm glad you could come."

"Wouldn't have missed it for the world. It's not every day you turn thirteen."

As they passed the front door, a loud knock startled them both.

"Wonder who that is? The party doesn't start for hours."

Becca opened the door. Mac stood on the front porch.

"Excuse me, is Dr. Walsh here?"

Cissy stepped out from behind Rebecca.

"Mac. What are you doing here?"

"I came to give you an update on your truck. The mechanic said he should be able to fix it today and they can bring it out to you in the morning. Ok?"

Rebecca's eyebrows rose. "Fixed? Why did it need to be fixed? What happened to it?"

"I had a small accident on the way here and Detective MacKellar kindly came to my aid."

"Do tell," responded Rebecca, icicles dripping from her voice. "And you were going to tell me... when?"

"It wasn't anything and I didn't want to spoil the party. I wasn't hurt."

"Right, but you could have been. Come in, Detective MacKellar. It's my twin daughters' birthday today. We were on our way to the kitchen to inspect the cakes. Since my friend forgot to mention such a trivial

81

incident, perhaps you would be so kind as to enlighten me." Rebecca, nose in the air, turned and marched toward the kitchen, the sound of her heels reverberating on the tile foyer.

"Sorry," whispered Mac as he slouched past Cissy.

"Thanks, Buddy," she mumbled as she followed the procession to the back of the house.

Once seated at the table, Rebecca spoke. "Alright. Spill. What happened?"

Cissy told Rebecca about her drive. "Nothing to worry about."

"Nothing to worry about? Didn't you just have the truck in for maintenance?"

"Last week."

"And why would the brakes fail now?"

"I don't know. Maybe they missed something."

Mac spoke up. "Actually, I know why. Cissy, your brake line was cut."

"What?" Cissy and Rebecca said in unison.

"It's what I was coming to tell you. Our guys went over the car, and they found a small slit in the brake line. By the time you got to Chalk Lake Road, your brakes would have failed."

"Why would anyone want the brakes to fail?"

"My guess is we hit a nerve with our announcement of the autopsy. Assumed her death would be put down as natural causes. Looks like we may find an outside cause after all."

Both women sat back in their chairs and looked at each other.

"I don't like the sound of this. Cissy, you can't do the autopsy."

"Don't be ridiculous, Becca. It's my job. Of course, I'll do it. I'll be more careful when I travel home. Once it's done, I pose no harm to anyone."

"That's why I'll be going home with you tomorrow and we'll be putting a guard in place at your condo until after it's completed," Mac said.

"Ridiculous. I'll be fine."

"Sorry. You don't get a vote. I don't need the best coroner in the region bumped off because I neglected to protect her."

Cissy leaned back in her chair, crossed her arms, and frowned.

Rebecca saw the stubborn set of her jaw and stood up. "Well, Detective MacKellar –"

"Call me Mac, please."

"Ok, Mac. I'm Becca. Would you care to stick around for the party? I know my family would love to meet you and it would give you time to sort things out with Cissy."

"I appreciate the invite, Becca, but I've gotta get back to the office." Mac stood and held out his hand. Becca took it in hers. "It's been a pleasure meeting you. I'll be back in the morning, Cissy."

"Hrrmph," replied Cissy.

Mac winked at Becca, turned, and walked out of the room.

Becca turned to Cissy. "You want to talk about it now? You should have told me this morning."

"There wasn't time. Besides, like I said, you've got enough going on today. You didn't need anything else to worry about and I know you. You would've stewed about it all day and spoiled the fun."

"I would not!"

"Yes, you would. But one thing I didn't share earlier is what happened when the car became airborne." Cissy told Becca about the strange light under the car and how it floated. "Then it went away once I landed. Very strange. Wonder if Martha's hanging around. If so, I'm grateful to her."

"Another ghost? I haven't seen one since Annie left."

"I know. Don't think I'll share it with Mac though. Probably freak him out. Not big on the supernatural."

"Well, if you need anyone to talk to him, I'm available."

"Thanks. I might have to take you up on that."

Chapter Twenty-One

arkness permeated the corridor. Tiny fissures of fear prickled the nape of her neck. Waiting as her eyes grew accustomed to the gloom, she stood in silence, ears opened on high alert. Could she hear breathing behind her or was it only sounds from the old furnace? Sweat dripped down between her shoulder blades like a melting icicle. Her hands burned as ice water filled her veins and flowed up her arms. Run. Frenetic energy coursing through her body, she ran down the hall, through the swinging doors and into the morgue. Her hand found the light switch and slapped it on. Nothing. Only suffocating darkness. She could feel a sinister presence in the room. She inhaled frigid air which had the tang of the metallic aftertaste of anesthesia. Her lungs felt like they were being squeezed by a bagpiper and a squeal came out of her airway. Who wanted to kill her? Why?

Cissy thrashed in the bed, discarding the covers, and vaulted to a sitting position. Heart racing several seconds passed before her confused mind sorted out her surroundings. Birds busy with their morning activities and the warm breeze wafting in through the open window roused Cissy from her nightmare. Gulping the air, she lay back on the bed trying to calm herself. Becca's. Right. She was here for the weekend. Only a nightmare. Long breath in; long breath out. Repeat her morning mantra. Again. With a gentle rhythm, her breathing returned to normal. Time to get up and face the day. Ugh. Mac was coming this morning. While she looked forward to seeing him, having him follow her home like a child was not how she wished to establish their relationship. Relationship? What relationship? If she were honest with herself, she'd admit she'd been thinking about it for some time. Don't go there. Cissy threw her legs over the edge of the bed and stomped to the bathroom. Once showered and dressed, she made her way to the kitchen.

Becca was up. Dressed in jeans, sweatshirt, rubber boots and a sun hat tied under her chin, she had been outside.

"What time is it?"

"Ten-thirty."

"Already? Again? Why didn't you wake me?"

"And have you grumpier than you are now? I don't think so. Here. Have your coffee."

"I'm not grumpy."

"Ya, right, girlfriend. You keep thinking it. Maybe you'll believe it. You're not usually this bad. What happened?"

"Crazy nightmare." Cissy explained to Becca what had awakened her. "It's nuts. The morgue was straight out of Frankenstein. Our new facilities are light and airy. Horrible. I felt like I had a million bugs crawling all over me." She shivered. "Ugh."

"Probably stirred up from your accident Friday night. You be careful going home."

"Mac's going to follow me. I'll be fine. Makes me feel like a baby who needs a babysitter. Not the impression I'd like to give him."

"Oh, you *do* want to make an impression."

"Not as a helpless female, I don't."

"Don't be ridiculous. I'm quite sure he sees you as a strong woman. I, for one, am glad he's going with you. Make sure you call me when you get home."

"I will. What's on the agenda for this morning?"

"Weeding's all done. I'm gonna take the dog food out to the kennels, feed the dogs, let them out in their run area and clean up their sleeping quarters. You wanna come?"

"Absolutely. Gives me one more chance to see the new pups you rescued from the mill."

The two friends picked up the food and equipment needed and spent a fun morning sharing and teasing each other. It was about two-thirty when they heard cars pulling up to the house. Cissy spotted Mac in his car, a man driving her truck and another man driving a tow truck. Once parked, Mac climbed out and walked over to the women.

"Afternoon, ladies."

"Afternoon to you, too."

Mac led the way over to Cissy's pickup and introduced her to the other two men.

"Bob, this is Dr. Cecelia Walsh, the owner."

"Afternoon, Dr. Walsh. Your truck is good to go. Mac here filled you in on the problem. Tiny leak in your brake line, but it's all fixed now. If you'll sign these papers, we'll get outta your hair."

"Thanks, Bob. You're sure the brake line was cut? No chance of a stone chip or something?"

"Yes, ma'am. Definitely cut. Although, when Mac told me what happened, I was surprised. Landing in a field the way you did, there should have been front-end damage but there wasn't a mark on her. You're one lucky lady.

Cissy glanced over at Becca and grinned. She signed the bill and retrieved her keys from Bob. "What's the charge?"

"No charge. Been taken care of," said Bob. He gave her a copy of the contract and with a wave he and his partner got into the tow truck and drove away.

"Did you pay for this?" asked Cissy, turning to face Mac.

"Yeah. Well, I was the one who held you up at the estate. You could have been seriously hurt. Least I could do."

"You don't know the leak happened at the Bancroft Estates. It could've been any time. I'll write you a cheque as soon as we get to my place."

"We do know it occurred at the Bancroft Estates. I went back and examined the area where you parked. The brake fluid had soaked into the ground. Left quite a stain."

Cissy frowned. "Guess someone doesn't want the autopsy done. Don't they realize even with me out of the picture it would be done anyway?"

"Doubt they thought that far. My guess it was spur of the moment rage. Didn't expect an autopsy. Thought they'd have lots of time to find the will and destroy it. What happened to it? Where did it go? No one seems to know. Everyone claims they didn't see it again after Winslow handed it to Martha. I don't buy it. It's gotta be around and one of them knows where. Anyway, are you ready? I'd like to get back to the office to go over the testimonies again."

"I'm ready, but you really don't have to come with me. I'm fine on my own."

"Let's go."

Mac took Cissy arm and walked her to the door of the house. She shook off his hand and pushed through the entrance. Becca strolled up to him. "You know, you'd get a lot farther with her if you'd simply ask instead of ordering her. Just sayin'."

"I don't order."

"Really? You don't hear yourself, do you?"

"I hear myself fine. It's been nice meeting you, Rebecca. I'd still like to hear your story."

"Anytime."

Mac put on his sunglasses, turned around and walked to his car. He tapped his fingers on the steering wheel while glancing toward the house. A few minutes later, Cissy opened the door and stepped out onto the porch, clutching her overnight bag. She gave Becca a hug. "Bye, sister. I'll call when I get home, although I don't think I should have any more problems," she said as she rolled her eyes.

"Bye, Sweetie. We'll talk soon."

Cissy turned on her heel and pulling the luggage behind her, stomped to the truck. After storing her suitcase, she climbed in. Starting it, she gave a final wave and drove down the driveway. Mac followed closely behind all the way to Cissy's home in Brooklin. Using the remote, Cissy opened the garage door and parked inside. Mac pulled up behind her and stopped. Cissy retrieved her bag as Mac removed his sunglasses and walked up to her. He tried to take the valise, but Cissy stopped him. "I'm quite capable of looking after my own suitcase, Detective."

"Suit yourself. Just trying to be a gentleman."

"As you can see, I'm home fine. You can go now."

"Dr. Walsh, I would be derelict in my duty if I didn't make sure your home was secure. May I please come in?"

"Oh, fine," said Cissy testily. She walked to the front door and opened it.

"Wait here," ordered Mac. He held her back as he went inside. Everything was quiet. He examined the house quickly and walked back to the door. "All clear. You can come in now."

Cissy entered the house and looked around. Everything was as she had left it. She let out a breath she hadn't realized she was holding.

"Thanks for the care, Mac. I didn't realize I was as anxious as I was. Never encountered anything like this before. I'm a little rattled."

"No problem. Gotta go. Lock your door and if anything bothers you, call."

"Thanks. I will."

Mac looked deeply into her grey eyes. He felt like he was being drawn into a churning mist which would enclose them in their own world. Just one touch. He reached out to caress her face, leaning in to taste her. He drew back at the last second.

"Um. See ya," he said as he retrieved his sunglasses from his pocket and put them on.

"Yeah," whispered Cissy a little dazed.

Mac walked back to his car and climbed in. Giving her one last wave, he backed out of the driveway and drove down the road. Cissy stood staring at the empty space where he had been, her hand brushing the cheek he'd been about to touch. A breeze brought her out of her reverie. Straightening her shoulders, she grabbed her suitcase, entered the hall, closed, and locked the door. Propelling herself forward, she strode into her living room and collapsed into her favorite chair, pulling out her cell as she plopped down.

"Hey, girlfriend. I'm home."

"Great. How was the ride."

"Totally uneventful. I knew it would be."

"Cissy, you don't know what the killer is thinking. What if whoever it was tries again?"

"Nothing's gonna happen. Somebody panicked at the thought of the autopsy, so they tried to stop it. Once they realize it isn't going to be stopped, they'll move on."

"Don't be too sure. They may want revenge for even suggesting a post-mortem and not ruling it a natural death. You don't know whose plans you spoiled by doing this. I wish you weren't involved."

"Silly. I'll be fine. And if I'm not, now you can see the other side, I'll visit you from the Great Beyond."

"Don't even joke about it."

"Lighten up. Look, we'll get together next week, and have a chat."

Chapter Twenty-Two

As Cissy predicted, nothing untoward happened during the rest of the weekend. Monday morning, cirrus clouds drifted across the blue sky like wisps of angel hair spread across a Christmas tree. A soft breeze ruffled Cissy's tresses as she stepped out of her car in front of the Forensic Service and Coroner's Complex in Toronto. A smile curved her lips, and her heart skipped a beat. She never tired of looking at this edifice. Opened in 2013, the 50,000-square meter center was five stories high with an underground holding six vehicle bays for the examination of vehicles involved in crime. Designed by Stantec Architects, it resembled a modern office complex, but the equipment housed in the building rivaled the state-of-the-art facility at the FBI's Quantico. Gone were the dim light and crowded conditions of the old building. The new autopsy room to which she was headed, was open and airy, with natural light and lots of space to move around the table. There was even a large room where ten autopsies could be performed at the same time, in the case of large-scale disasters or epidemics. A modern lab with the latest in appliances such as dozens of adjustable "snorkels" used for purging the air of toxic gases produced by mass spectrometer gas chromatographs, machines used to identify drugs, toxins, and accelerants.

Cissy walked into the atrium and up to the second floor to change into her scrubs. She then returned to the first floor and entered the autopsy suite.

"Good morning, Anita," she said to the Forensic Technology Assistant.

"Good morning, Dr. Walsh. Everything's all set."

"Okey dokey. Let's get this show on the road."

Cissy moved to the table and began the post-mortem.

"Well, Martha. What do you want to tell me today?"

Completing the autopsy, Cissy straightened her spine and stretched. "Okay, Anita. I'm done here. I'm going back to the office to finish the other reports and write down my observations for this one."

"Thanks, Dr. Walsh. I'll look after Mrs. Bancroft."

As she left the autopsy suite, she put her hand on the small of her back and made her way up to her second-floor office. Entering the room, she took off her cap, sat at the desk and closed her eyes. She clicked a remote on her desk and soothing music filled the air. After she relaxed for a few moments, she reached into her pocket and pulled out her cell.

"Mac. It's Cissy. I've completed the physical autopsy. No, I didn't find anything suspicious. The heart was normal. No disease. She was a healthy seventy-five-year-old woman and except for severe arthritis, I would have expected her to live for quite a while. We'll have to wait for the results from the toxicology and tissue sample report before I have anything definitive. I've put a rush on them, but it will still take a while. I'll release the body for burial shortly. For now, we'll inform the family the results are inconclusive. We'll know more when the final results are in. In the meantime, I suggest you continue investigating."

When Cissy released Martha's body, it was taken to the mortuary and prepared for burial. The day of the funeral dawned cool and cloudy. A stiff breeze scattered the fallen leaves in front of Andrew and Vanessa as they approached the chapel. Vanessa shivered as she clutched her coat closer and put her head down against the wind. A member of the funeral staff opened the front door and ushered them into the main viewing room. The casket had pride of place at the center front, banked

91

by four large baskets of flowers. A spray of roses marked with ribbons which read "Mother" and "Grandmother" lay on the closed section. The unfurled Canadian flag stood guard to the left. Three rows of fifteen pews filled the room. The body reposed peacefully on the white plush velvet interior of the coffin. Made of solid mahogany with gold trim, it gleamed with a high gloss finish.

The two spirits hovered near the front of the casket. Martha gazed at the shell which once housed her spirit.

"Wow," she chuckled. "I haven't looked this good in years! Should've used this gal for my hair and makeup. Look at the fancy casket. Hrmph. No expense spared; I see."

Hearing voices at the back of the room, Martha and Gladys focused their attention there.

Andrew and Vanessa walked up the aisle with the director of the funeral home.

"Yes, Mr. Bancroft, all the arrangements have been made as you requested. The service starts at eleven, after which a luncheon will be prepared in our Renaissance room. Later, for those who wish, we will form a processional to take your mother to the family plot in Orchard Park for the committal service. I trust you will find everything satisfactory."

The trio stopped in front of the casket. Looking down on his mother, Andrew's face was hard and cold. His blue eyes were inscrutable, and his mouth pursed in a thin line.

Vanessa grabbed his arm. "Oh, look, Andy. Doesn't she look wonderful? The blue dress was the right choice. I wasn't sure but laying against the white velvet, she looks just like she's sleeping. Oh, dear, where's my Kleenex? I can't believe she's gone. I'm going to sit down. I've never seen a dead person before and I –". Vanessa took the tissue from her purse, dabbed her eyes, turned, and sat down in the front pew reserved for family.

"I'm going to leave you now," said the director. "I will be downstairs in the office and my colleague will be right out front in the

92

foyer. If you require any assistance whatsoever, please send a family member to find us. We'll be happy to be of service."

"What? Oh, yes, Mr. Holmes. Thank you for your service."

Mr. Holmes nodded to Andrew and quietly withdrew.

Andrew gripped the side of the coffin, his knuckles turning white and the pulse in his temple visibly throbbing. Staring at his dearly departed, he whispered "Why, Mother? Why couldn't you love me as much as you loved Edward? You even loved my son more than me. What did I ever do to make you hate me so much? It was bad enough you took Ruth's side against me in the divorce, but to give everything to my son instead of me? It's intolerable! Thank goodness the will wasn't signed."

Martha gasped. "No. He's not right. I do love him as much as Ed."

"Apparently, he doesn't think so," replied Gladys.

"How could he not know? He was my baby boy. My youngest. He wasn't as emotionally strong as Ed, so I tried not to pamper him. Wanted him to toughen up and be a man."

"Be a man. When he was a little boy? How?"

"You know. Stand up for himself. Not cry at the least little thing. He was a bit of a crybaby. Others teased him about it. I needed to harden him. Prepare him for life. It was for his own good."

"You couldn't leave life to teach him and just be there when he needed you? What about Jared? You certainly seem to favour him."

"Only because he's going to look after the ranch."

"Be honest with yourself. You're sure it's the only reason?"

Martha was silent for a moment. "I dunno, maybe there's more. He's so much like my Bobby; I did tend to indulge him. Honestly didn't think anyone would notice. Obviously, I was wrong. If I was wrong about that, what else was I blind to? Can it be my fault Drew is the way he is?"

"No. We're responsible for our own choices. Only Drew's answerable for his decisions. Not you. But it's too bad you didn't sort it out before you died. You might've had a decent relationship."

"You're right. Looks like I still have a lot to learn."

"Don't we all," replied Gladys.

Turning her attention to the back of the room, Martha said, "Oh, look. Ruth and Charli have come. I'm glad."

Gladys saw a woman in her late forties approach the casket. She was about five and a half feet tall with short hair the color of caramel peppered with streaks of white. Her warm brown eyes were alight with intelligence and humor. When she smiled, tiny lines creased their edges. Beside her stood a young woman about twenty-five, a younger version of her mother. She was taller but had the same qualities of character shining from identical brown eyes.

"Hello, Andrew."

"Ruth. I didn't expect you here."

"She was my mother-in-law and Charli's grandmother. Where else would we be? She looks nice. I hope she died peacefully."

"Why wouldn't she?"

"Well, Jared said the Friday meeting didn't go well and the police have been asking questions. You were upset with her."

"It's bad enough my son and daughter have betrayed me by working on the ranch, but to turn the estate into an animal sanctuary is crazy. We could sell it for millions and develop it for people."

"You never could see the bigger picture, could you? It's not about the money. It's about the future. Not building on the Moraine. Preserving food and water for our kids and grandkids."

"Bullshit."

"So you say. By the way, your son and daughter are highly respected in their chosen fields and thoroughly enjoy what they are doing. Don't push it or you'll end up losing both."

"Jared, a vet and Charlotte, a naturopath or whatever the hell it is she's doing. They both could have been executives in the company and been set for life."

"Dad, this is not the time or place," interrupted Charli. "Mom, we should find out seats. The service will be starting shortly and there is a lineup waiting to pay their respects to Grandma."

Charli took hold of her mother's arm and after kissing her dad's cheek she led Ruth to their seats. Andrew took one last look at his mother and turned to find his own seat.

"Well," said Gladys. "It's nice to see both Charli and Ruth."

"Ruth is a lovely woman and Charli is special to me. I'll never understand why Drew left Ruth and took up with... with...," Martha huffed.

"You've never given Vanessa much of a chance, have you? Is Ruth such a paragon of virtue?"

"I thought so. They seemed perfect for each other."

"Maybe not so much. Why blame Vanessa? It's as much Drew's fault as hers."

"She seduced him."

"Hmmm. Positive, are you?"

"Why else would he leave his family and chase after her?"

"Maybe because he and Ruth weren't on the same page anymore? Or maybe he's a narcissist who couldn't keep it in his pants?"

"I tried to put a stop to it."

"You did. Let's refresh your memory."

Gladys took them back to a day long before Robert died. The scene showed Martha many years earlier seated at Robert's desk in the library.

Chapter Twenty-Three

Alone in the house, Martha signed onto the Internet. Reaching for her cup of tea, she knocked over the desk lamp. As she picked it up, she noticed there was a piece of paper stuck to the underside of the base.

"Well, what have we here?"

On closer inspection, she saw Drew's ID and password for his email account. Little sparks tingled her fingers. She chortled to herself. "Foolish boy."

In the past few months, whenever she and Bobby visited at Drew and Ruth's home, tempers between the two appeared strained. Ruth told her he'd been coming home later at night and was taking more and more "business trips" out of town. Involved in the company, Martha knew there had been no junkets lately, so where was he going? Bobby had warned her to keep out of it, but she couldn't. He was her son and by God, if he were up to no good, she'd soon put a stop to it. She wouldn't stand by and let him soil the family name. She privately asked questions at the office and did a little snooping. Now his password had literally fallen into her lap, she took it as a sign she should take a peek at his emails to see what was going on.

Martha signed into his email and scanned the messages. As she did her heart skipped a beat and a wave of dizziness spread from her face down to her toes. Her ice-cold hands started to shake. Tons of messages, some explicit, outlining a whole sordid affair with the slut, Vanessa Beaumont. She was a waitress in the private boxes at the racetrack. A waitress! Martha knew Vanessa was only looking for a good time. She didn't care who she suckered into her web. The last message said they would be meeting at her place at two o'clock today.

Fury flooded Martha's body like a river of molten lava. She looked at her watch. The hands stood at one fifteen. She would put an end to this NOW!

Springing from the chair, Martha raced out into the hall, picked up her keys from the table at the door and flew out of the house. She opened the garage and climbed into her little Audi sports car. Backing out of the driveway, she peeled rubber and raced into town. As she reached Vanessa's Street, she slowed to a crawl looking for Drew's car. She spotted it parked a couple of blocks from the house. So much for discretion. Her cheeks burned in humiliation. *Does he really think he could park this close and not have someone notice?* She left her car in front of the house and marched up to the entrance. Lifting the knocker, she hammered on the door and stood waiting for Vanessa to answer.

Vanessa, dressed in a silk and feather dressing gown with dainty pink slippers on her feet, opened to see an enraged woman standing on her front porch. With a sneer on her face, Martha looked her up and down. "Get that son of mine out here this minute." Vanessa's eyes widened and her mouth dropped open. She stumbled back into the foyer. Andy had assured her no one knew of their little afternoon romps. "Yes, Mrs. Bancroft, right away." She slammed the door in Martha's face and ran back into the house. "Andy, your mother's here."

Andrew was coming out of the bedroom, his shirt unbuttoned, pants unzipped and in bare feet. "Shit. How'd she find me? Better see what she wants." Andrew zipped his pants and walked to the entryway. He took a deep breath and swung the door open.

"Mother. What the hell are you doing here?"

"Watch your language. I am your mother."

Andrew straightened his shoulders and glared at Martha. Jaw clenched, he replied, "When you show up at my friend's home and make a scene, I'll speak to you as you deserve. What do you want?"

Martha pushed to her full five foot, eight inches as she gave her son a withering scowl. "We have a good name in this town, and I will not have it destroyed by you having a sordid affair. That tramp you've been

97

sniffing around is just after your money. Well, she won't get any of mine, so you're on your own there. Now, get dressed properly and go home to your family."

"Watch what you say. Vanessa is my friend and I'll not let you or anyone else insult her. I am not going to discuss family business on the front steps. Go home. I'll be there shortly. We can discuss this in a civilized manner."

He slammed the door in his mother's face and walked back into the bedroom to speak to Vanessa. "I'd better go, Nessa," he said. "Mother is on the warpath, and she may try to cut me off or get me removed from the board. I need her to calm down. I'll be back later, and we can finish where we left off."

"I heard what she said. I'm not a tramp and I'm not after your money. I love you. Why is she angry with me Andy Panda? I make you happy, don't I?"

"You make me happy, my gorgeous girl. I can't wait to get you back into bed."

Vanessa giggled. "You think she'd be happy I'm making her son happy. I miss you already. Come back soon and I'll give you a special treat."

"Ahhh, you're killing me, but I gotta go. Keep the bed warm and I'll be back as soon as I can get my mother off my back."

The scene faded. Gladys and Martha returned to their current state.

"Whoa. What an experience. Funny, when you're in a body, you can close off the effect of your words or actions. In my self-righteousness, I didn't see how I made them feel. On this side, nothing's blocked. You feel what your attitude does to people."

Gladys spoke. "Do you think it was the right way to handle the situation?"

"Yeah, at the time. Now... not so much. He was a grown man and had his own path. Bobby was right. I shouldn't have interfered, but I wanted to protect him."

"Think deeper."

98

"I thought she was after his money and would dump him as soon as she got her hands on it."

"Deeper."

Martha was silent for a few minutes thinking about what she had seen and heard. "I see. You're right. I was more concerned about how the affair would appear to our friends and how it would affect me. I took pride in our social standing, and this would put a crimp in it."

"Bingo. And how'd it work for you?"

"We had a huge row, and he didn't speak to me for months. His father was drawn in and, since he'd already told me to mind my own business, he took Drew's side, and we ended up in a fight."

"Was she really so bad?"

"Well, she wasn't up to our standards. After Drew's divorce, they flew down to Vegas and got married in some tawdry chapel. I was surprised they didn't have Elvis perform the ceremony."

"If she was so 'lower class', why didn't you help her instead of criticizing her?"

"I don't know."

"A little too close to home, maybe? But why blame her? It was as much his responsibility as it was hers."

"She lured him away with her body and…and."

"Quit harping on that. If his marriage were as solid as you seem to think, another woman couldn't have lured him away no matter how gorgeous she was. Who are you really angry with?"

"What do you mean?"

"Vanessa provided a good target, so you don't have to face what's really bugging you. I remember another young woman who came from the wrong side of the tracks to scrape and climb her way to the top of the social ladder."

Martha looked at Gladys and then at the floor.

"Oh, well."

"Let's go back a little further, shall we?"

A new scene presented a young Martha on her way to school. Martha and Gladys became silent witnesses to the action.

Chapter Twenty-Four

A soft breeze with a hint of the winter to come rustled the leaves as Martha made her way to school. Shivering she pulled her jacket tighter to her body. How she hated this jacket. It was so last year and the year before if truth were told. It was a little snug across the shoulders and wouldn't close properly now she'd filled out. Her face set in a scowl; she kicked a rock on the sidewalk. Her mom mended every hole with a flower. Soon the jacket would resemble a freaking garden. While her mother's work was beautiful and the jacket was one of a kind, it still shouted 'poor girl'.

"Might as well wear a sign saying, 'POOR GIRL HERE'", she muttered.

This was her fourth year at Humber High. It was a large sprawling structure in the middle of Toronto and had fifteen hundred students. Out of all those kids she had to be stuck in class with Susan Harmon.

Rich snob.

Susan was the daughter of a well-known doctor. They lived in Forest Hill, and he could well afford to send his daughter to Branksome Hall as most of his colleagues did, but the good doctor decided he wanted his offspring to learn the value of money and make her realize she was no better than those who weren't as fortunate. Unfortunately, after several huge temper tantrums which didn't move her father one bit, Susan found by attending a public high school she was able to gather a small clique of girls who would do anything to be in her circle. She also discovered her penchant for making caustic remarks about other students brought gales of laughter from her so called new friends thus placating her bruised ego. Martha had wandered into Susan's range of sight at the end of last year, making her already lonely life intolerable. She was almost finished. Come June, she'd be out of here and it would be bye-bye Susan.

Keep your head down and stay out of her way.

No such luck. As Martha approached the front steps of the school, who should be standing at the top but Susan and her cronies. Martha hugged her books a little closer to her chest and eyes downcast, started up the broad, concrete stairs.

"Look who's back. The garden princess. Still wearing that raggedy ol' jacket?" Susan called. Her friends stared at Martha and giggled.

So much for avoiding her, thought Martha. "Shut up, Susan," she said.

"Ohh, dear. I've upset the princess. And if I don't, what do you intend to do about it?" she smirked.

As Martha was about to reply, Robert Bancroft came up the stairs beside her. "Hey, Martha. Good to see you. My mom wants you to come to my place after school. She's got some stuff for your mom. If you want, I'll wait for you at the front doors, and we can walk together."

Martha smiled up at him. "Great, Bobby. Thanks."

"Okay. See ya." Bobby ran up the rest of the stairs and into the school.

Martha looked over at her nemesis. Susan's face had turned a mottled red, eyebrows drawn together in a frown and her eyes flashed fire. "Keep away from him. Understand. A little nobody like you isn't going to spoil my plans. He's mine," she whispered as Martha walked past.

Martha turned and glared at her. "I don't like threats. Stay away from me and we'll get along fine. Get in my way and you'll be sorry." She pushed past the group and strode through the front doors.

As the image faded, Martha and Gladys found themselves back at the funeral parlor.

"There. You see? She was a horrible person. Even after Bobby and I got married she tried to lure him away from me. Arrrggghh. I hate home wreckers. Winning is all they care about. It doesn't matter if the object of their attention is married with a family. They only care about themselves."

"I do see."

"Then you understand why I'm angry with Vanessa. She ruined my son's marriage and broke up his home."

"Did she?"

"Yes!"

"Or are you afraid to face our own insecurity because you've never felt good enough for Bobby? Tell me, did he ever return Susan's flirtations?"

"No! Definitely not. How can you suggest such a thing?"

"You've thought about it though, haven't you?"

Martha's light dimmed and she looked at the ground. "I guess," she whispered. "After all, she was beautiful and from a wealthy family. I was a nobody. There was a time after the children were born. He went away on a business trip. It was how he acted when he got back. More distant and distracted. I convinced myself it was a crucial time for the company to really make it big, but I was never sure. I saw Susan a few weeks later and she had the cat that swallowed the canary look on her face. Came over to me gushing with bonhomie. I didn't say anything to Bobby and after a couple of months, things got back to normal, but I was never sure."

"Yet, you never did blame Bobby. Instead, you stuffed your resentment deep inside and when Vanessa came along, you had a target readymade."

"No, I would never do that!"

"Martha," said Gladys softly.

"I… hmmm." Martha was silent for a while, pondering what she had seen and felt. "Guess so," she muttered. "Not what I intended before I was born, but I can see how it happened."

"You remember your blueprint?"

"This part. A few centuries back, I incarnated as male. A hometown hero loved by everyone. Planning this past life, I wanted feel vulnerable. See if I could be loving while not being as secure with love. Once I got here, I forgot why I'd wanted certain people to be in my life and I made mistakes."

"Cool. That's a lesson the team will be able to use." Gladys looked around the funeral home. "Looks like everybody's left. Let's go join them."

Gladys and Martha left the parlor and traveled to the graveside.

Chapter Twenty-Five

The wind picked up as everyone arrived at the cemetery. People huddled together to keep warm. Martha and Gladys glided to the edge of the group. Percy stamped his feet.

"Really, Mother. Where is Uncle Andrew? I'm freezing. Can't we get this over with?"

"I know, my precious boy. If I'd known it would take this long, I wouldn't have come. Just a little longer. Must look the part of the grieving family, even if I'm glad to be rid of the old hag."

Percy snickered. "Yes. When we fight for our rightful inheritance, we wouldn't want the judge to think there was any discord, now would we?"

Adele giggled. "No, we would not."

Martha overheard their conversation and squirmed at the vehemence in their voices.

Where is Drew?

The Minister approached Adele.

"I'm sorry, Mrs. Bancroft, but we need to proceed."

"That's fine, Reverend. I have no idea what's keeping my brother-in-law. He should have been here by now. You can go ahead."

Reverend Small proceeded with the committal service. Just as the pastor concluded the prayers and the coffin was being lowered into the grave an SUV came screeching to a halt at the curb.

"Wait, Wait," called a female voice. The passenger's side door flung open, and Vanessa jumped out. "We're here. I'm sorry we were so long. I lost my bag and Andy was searching for it. We finally found it beneath one of the pews at the chapel. How it ever got there, I don't know. I

105

wasn't anywhere near that seat."

The whole time she was chattering, Vanessa was rushing to the grave.

"Good grief. Will that child never learn? Look at those heels. She's going to break her neck wearing those things out here," Martha exclaimed.

As Martha was speaking to Gladys, Vanessa reached the edge of the grave. Her heel caught in the soft ground throwing her off balance. Swaying with the force of the abrupt stop, she put out her hands to steady herself and toppled into the open grave.

"Aaaahhhhhhh"

"Vanessa."

Andrew ran up to the grave and peered in. There she was, sprawled on top of the casket her one foot shoeless and her hat lying askew on the back of her head.

"Andy," came the muffled voice. "Get me out of here." She pushed herself up into a seating position and wailed. "Help. Oh, no. I'm on top of Mother Bancroft. This gives me the willies. Get me out."

"Gladys, we have to help the poor girl," cried Martha rushing to the open grave.

Once recovered from their shock, Adele and Percy glanced at each other. Turning her head and covering her mouth, she coughed and cleared her throat. Although his eyes were downcast, Percy's shoulders were bouncing up and down as he clasped his hands behind his back.

Andrew looked at his nephew, his eyes black with rage.

"Percy, do something useful for once in your life. Jared, you, and your cousin give me a hand."

Both men walked to the grave and with an energy boost from the two spirits, they managed to pull her up out of the hole to firm ground. She lay panting on all fours. She began to cry. Andrew knelt beside his wife and took her in his arms. Vanessa turned her head into the side of his neck and sobbed.

"I'm so sorry. I've made a mess of things again. How you must hate me."

"Shhh, sweetheart. It's ok. I don't hate you. How could I hate my Nessa?" Andrew put his hand underneath her chin and lifted her head. He looked into her eyes and smiled. Lifting a gloved hand, he tucked a strand of hair behind her ear and straightened her hat. "I could never hate you," he said kissing her forehead. "C'mon let's go back to the house and get you cleaned up."

Andrew stood and held out his hands to his wife. Reaching for them, she rose to stand beside him. He turned to the rest of the crowd and said, "I apologize for the interruption. My wife and I are returning to the house. If you can, we would like you to follow to reminisce about my mother's life and legacy and to enjoy some light refreshments. Thank you."

Adele and Percy looked at the ground as the couple passed them. Jared, Charli, and their mother watched with sad eyes as their dad and his wife strode to the waiting car. The rest of the guests stood quietly by while Andrew and Vanessa drove away. Once they were gone, the people all began to chatter.

"How very typical of the lower class," Percy whispered to his mother.

"She does provide some comic relief," said Adele. "I certainly won't ever forget this funeral. Poor Andrew. How humiliating," she snickered.

"Come along, Mother. Let's see what she can come up with for an encore." Percy took his mother's arm and led her to the funeral car. The rest of the guests took their cue from them and soon everyone was gone from the cemetery."

"That was awful," said Martha. "That poor girl. She was mortified and then to listen to Percy and Adele."

"You would have sided with them a few days ago."

"No. I wouldn't have said anything."

"You wouldn't have to. Your frown and demeanor would speak volumes."

Martha was silent for a long time. "You're right. I see now how my actions, or lack thereof, certainly haven't helped her."

"Drew handled himself well. He really does love the girl. That should please you."

"Yeah, it does. We could've had the kind of family I really wanted if I hadn't been so self-righteous."

"Don't be so hard on yourself. This was only one small part of your life. You did lots of stuff I'm sure you'll be happy with, but we must get home first to have your life review. We can't get to that until we finish here. Let's get back to the house and see what we can find out."

Chapter Twenty-Six

The atmosphere at the Bancroft Estate was solemn as befitting a funeral reception. Friends and family gathered in the living room to share memories of Martha over cups of coffee, tea and hors d'oeuvres. Martha and Gladys, cloaked as orbs of light, took up their spots in the drapes. Jared stood at the picture window looking out at the garden. A long-time neighbor, Mrs. Carlisle, approached.

"I'm so sorry for your loss, Dr. Bancroft."

"Thank you, Mrs. Carlisle."

"She was such a stalwart in the community. I don't know what we will do without her leadership on the 'Save the Moraine' committee. She was passionate about saving the land and the water. Do you know what will happen to the ranch? You're not going to sell, are you?"

"It's a little up in the air at the moment."

"Oh, dear. I thought she had it all wrapped up. I do hope those horrible developers don't get their hands on it."

"The developers? Have they been around to your place as well?"

"Oh, yes. Mind you, I gave them what for, just like your grandmother. Sell them my land for a housing development? Not in this lifetime. But now Martha is gone, if the estate is sold to them, I guess I won't have any other option. I certainly don't want to live next to a bunch of rowdy neighbors. That's one of the reasons I moved out here. To get away from crowded subdivisions. I love my land and don't want to move, but I'm not getting any younger. Oh, I'm going to miss Martha. She always knew what to do." Mrs. Carlisle's face scrunched up and she reached into her purse for a handkerchief. She dabbed her eyes and blew her nose.

Jared tried to comfort her. "I'm sure everything will be alright," he said. "It'll take a little time, as Grandma's death was unexpected, but I'm sure her wishes will be approved in the end."

"Yes, it was unexpected, wasn't it? Although, I guess at our age, you should surmise it could happen at any time. Do you know what happened?"

"We think it was a heart attack."

"Really? She never mentioned that she was having trouble with her heart. Perhaps she didn't know. I understand these things can come out of nowhere. Why, I remember a mutual friend who –"

"Excuse me, Mrs. Carlisle. I don't wish to be rude, but I must speak with my father before he leaves. Family business. You understand."

"Yes, of course. I didn't mean to monopolize your time. Oh, my, look at the hour. I must leave myself. Please give my condolences to your father. I'll stop by next week to see how everyone is getting along. You take care of yourself. I know you'll miss her dreadfully. Such a good boy." Mrs. Carlisle patted his cheek and took herself out of the room.

Jared rubbed his temple. How he hated these receptions, especially this one. He searched the room for his father. Seeing Andrew by the coffee stand, he ambled over to him.

"Dad."

"Jared."

"What happens now?"

"If you mean 'what do I intend to do about that blasted will', I don't know. The first thing we have to do is find it."

"What do you mean, 'find it'? Where did it go?" Jared asked.

"That's what I'd like to know. I talked to Tom, but he said he doesn't have it."

"True. Grandmother wanted to look at all her papers when she went to bed. She made Tom give them to her. He handed her an envelope, and she took it upstairs with her."

"No one has seen it since," Andrew said.

"It must be in her room."

"It isn't. I've searched high and low and can't find it. Tom says he never saw it when we found Mother the next morning. I've asked everyone else, and they all claim they never saw the papers after the meeting Friday night. So, where is it?"

"I don't know. I haven't seen the envelope since I saw it under Grandma's arm," Jared said.

"Since we can't find the new will, I presume the old one will be in effect, which suits me fine. I hope it's never found. Then we can stop all this sanctuary and 'save the land' nonsense and be practical."

"What do you mean?"

"I mean Adele and I will inherit under the old will and we both agree the best thing for this family and property is to sell a large portion of it to Fern Glen Developments and retain the rest for the family as a vacation home. We don't need all this land. We're not farmers and bringing more people out here would be good for the economy. It's a win/win all the way around."

"You can't do that. It's not what Grandma wanted. What about the Moraine? The developers won't be able to build here. It's too close. It won't be allowed." Jared's voice rose.

"Don't worry. There are ways around that little stipulation. A lot of builders have banded together and have clout with local and provincial people. It may take a while, but they'll get over that hurdle and you'll see homes here."

"Even if it destroys the water and the land?"

"Bullshit! Bunch of nonsense spouted by tree huggers." Andrew's volume matched his son's.

"You're wrong. Such a narrow-minded asshole. I'll fight you on this. That will has to be somewhere and I'm going to find it. I'm staying at the house until this is settled, but I will take it to the Supreme Court if I must. You won't get away with stopping Grandma's dream." Jared strode out of the house by way of his grandmother's sitting room and down to the barns.

111

Percy watched him from his corner of the room. Sidling up to his mother, he took her arm and steered her into the kitchen.

"Mother, we need to figure out a way to stay at the house for the next little while. I overheard Uncle Andrew and Jared arguing." He told Adele what he had discovered. "That twit is going to ruin everything if he finds the will. We must find and destroy it before Golden Boy does. I also want to keep an eye on Vanessa. She's acting weird. She knows something, but what? Do you think you could say that due to all the stress of these last few weeks, you really need to stay here to rest?"

"Excellent idea, my pet. The stress really has been too much for my heart and I do need to rest. It's quiet and peaceful here. Very conducive to healing. I will tell Andrew that we are staying, then we'll do whatever we can to find that will. It must be destroyed."

The duo went their separate ways. Adele, back into the living room to find Andrew and Percy, down to the library to snoop around.

Martha's light began to spark. "Did you hear what my lout of a son said?"

"Yes."

"I wish I'd told Vanessa to take it to Tom or the detective. I'm glad I told her not to tell Drew. He'll destroy it."

"But Tom will have copies."

"Yes, but none of them have been signed. It isn't valid if it isn't signed. Only the copy in the safe is valid. We must find a way to get it to the cop."

Chapter Twenty-Seven

T he warm October sunlight bathed the hallway as Adele eased open the door to her bedroom. Peering up and down, she cocked her ear, ready to pull back into the room if she heard footsteps on the stairs. The melody of birds filtered through the yawning window, but she heard no other sound.

Adele pushed the door wider and stepped out of her room. With the rug muffling her footsteps, she crept down the hallway to Percy's room and with her knuckles barely touching the door, she rapped and whispered, "Percy." After a few seconds, the door clicked open, and her son slid through the crack as he joined his mother. In silence, Percy shut the door.

The duo smiled at one another and made their way to Martha's room. Looking toward the staircase, Percy nodded to Adele, turned the doorknob, and slithered through the opening. He widened the entrance to let his mother in and then with delicate fingers pushed the door closed with a soft click.

Unbeknownst to the pair, two ghostly figures observed their antics and followed them into the room.

"They're going to try and find the will. We should be able to have some fun with this," said Martha with glee.

Percy leaned against the door. "Made it. I thought the rest of them would never leave."

"It would be like Vanessa to have forgotten one of her precious purses and come back for it," sniffed Adele.

"Honestly. It's a wonder she can dress herself in the morning," smirked Percy.

Adele snickered. "And her antics at the graveside. I was mortified. Silly woman. Wearing those impossibly high heels on that ground.

Mother Bancroft would roll over in her grave if she had seen it. So undignified. I felt sorry for your uncle. What he must put up with, Lord only knows, but that's his problem. Right now, let's find the will so we can put things back the way they should be."

"I was there, you stupid troll. Don't you dare speak for me and what I was feeling," shouted Martha, her energy sending out small sparks into the atmosphere.

"Why don't we start in the closet. I've always wanted to see in there and your grandmother would never let me. Now's my chance."

Adele strode to the large walk-in closet and flung the double door open. Her eyes widened at the size of the room, the array of clothes, shoes, purses, and other paraphernalia that had belonged to the dead woman.

"Good grief. Would you look at the size of this room. It's bigger than my first apartment!" Her heart pounded as she edged forward caressing each garment as she moved into the space. "Oh, Percy. Look at these dresses. It's too bad I have a more statuesque build than Martha as they would look gorgeous on me."

"Statuesque? Ha. Fat is even being polite for you lady," muttered Martha. "Get your grubby hands off my things."

"I wouldn't mind some of these accessories, myself. Look at these scarves and the turtleneck sweaters. She even has a couple of lovely jackets that would be perfect for my trip overseas. A few minor alterations. Yes, they would do nicely," he murmured fingering the material. "But first things first. We must find the will. Where could it be?"

"Would she hide it in a box? A shoe box? She certainly has enough of those."

"Do they really think I would be that stupid," muttered Martha.

"Let's start going through them. I'll pull them down from the shelf and you see what's inside."

Martha watched for a few moments as the two concentrated on their task. Percy grabbed a step stool stored in the room and handed his

114

mother shoe box after shoe box. Adele sat on a small chair made for trying on shoes, emptying the boxes, and examining them, then piling the ones she had finished with beside her. Martha focused her energy on a little brown fur hat situated on a shelf above Adele's head. Looking like a little brown rat, it slid along until it tipped off the shelf and landed on Adele's shoulder as Percy handed her another box. The box, shoes and tissue paper flew into the air as Adele screamed and jumped to her feet. "Get it off me," she screamed. Hands flailing, she jumped around trying to see what had landed on her. When she saw the brown fur on the floor among the shoes and boxes, she put her hand to her heart and swooned. "It's a rat! It's a rat!" Percy jumped down from the step stool and hurried to see where his mother was pointing. He picked it up. He went to Adele and took hold of her upper arms. "Mother. Mother, it's ok. It's not a rat. Look. It's an old hat. It's fine. Calm down." Adele glanced down at the hat and burst into tears.

"Having fun, are we?" asked Gladys.

"Oh, yes. Now what else can I do?"

"Rather childish, doncha think?"

"Yup and I love it. You have no idea how long I have wanted to do something like this."

"Seems to be a waste of time."

"Oh, lighten up. Just a little karma. Couldn't happen to a more deserving person."

Adele sat on the footstool for a few moments to collect herself. "How did it fall, Percy? There's no breeze in here."

"Maybe moving the shoe boxes shook the rack it was on."

"Maybe. Well, all the shoe boxes have been checked and there's nothing in them."

"We need to go over the whole room. If we start at the back and do each section methodically, we should be able to check everything in no time. Knock on walls in case she has a hiding place behind a hollow one. I've seen people in movies tape important documents on the backs of mirrors or under dresser drawers, so we have to look there as well."

"Ok, but we'd better hurry. We don't know how long the others will be away."

They moved to the dressing area of the closet. She took in the stylish boutique atmosphere. "Good heavens. It's like a Parisian couturier. And she couldn't spare us anymore than a couple of hundred thousand. I shall have to insist that this room is mine once we get the will sorted out."

"Not on your life," shouted Martha. "You will never have any of this."

"Mother. Look at this mirror. It's from the Tiffany silver antique collection. Be still my heart," exclaimed Percy patting his chest. Adele approached the triple mirror and examined it from top to bottom, but there was nothing attached to it. As she came around the front, she investigated the glass, smiling at her reflection. "Not too bad. Once I get some of these clothes altered to fit me, I shall be the height of fashion. Won't the girls be jealous at the bridge club." As she stood there, she thought she saw a tiny reflection of something moving behind her. Turning, she tripped over a small crease in the rug and stumbled onto a white leather tub chair. Landing with a whoosh, she looked back at the rug, but could see no crease in the carpet. Uneasiness prickled up her neck and her eyes darted back and forth. Her legs wobbling, she tried to stand and jumped when a scarf floated down from one of the hangers and landed at her feet. "Percy."

He rushed to her side. "Mother. What happened?"

"I don't know. I'm sure there was a crease in that rug, and I tripped on it, but it's not there now."

"This has been a little overwhelming for you. Perhaps you need to go back to your room."

"I think you're right."

Percy took his mother's arm and helped her to her feet. Leading her out of the dressing area, a filmy gray dress floated off the rack nearest her and covered her face. "Ah. Get it off me," she screamed, arms flailing.

"Stop, Mother, stop," said Percy trying to brush away the dress from his mother's face. Pushing it onto the floor, the pair dashed out of the closet and into the bedroom. Panting, they pushed the closet doors closed and leaned against them. "I'm sure the will must be somewhere else. Perhaps Thomas does have it. We'll check with him," said Adele. Straightening her clothes and gathering as much dignity as she could, she made her way to the bedroom door. As the two exited the room, a blast of frigid air blew the door shut behind them.

"Don't let the door hit you on your way out."

Peering at each other sideways, they hurried down the hall with Martha's faint laughter following close behind.

Chapter Twenty-Eight

Thomas Winslow was not a happy man. The sweat trickled down his handsome face. Sitting in his home office, he thought about the Friday dinner party and meeting at Martha Bancroft's place. What was he going to do? He had tried to convince Martha not to sign the new will.

He thought back to the Tuesday before the weekend.

He had been pouring over charts and graphs in his office, and deep in concentration on devising a new strategy for his gambling addiction, when the intercom jangled. His hand jerked as he spilled ink all over his lovely charts.

"Yes," he shouted.

"I'm sorry to disturb you, Mr. Winslow, but there are a Mr. Carter and Mr. Bales from Fern Glen Developments here. They insist on seeing you."

"That's quite all right, Kathy. Send them in."

Thomas cleared his desk in one fell swoop, shoving everything on it into a satchel under his desk. He then straightened his tie, wiped his brow, and smoothed his hair. As the door opened, he closed his computer, thrust his papers into a drawer and moved to the credenza.

Two men entered the office. The first man was tall and lean, immaculately dressed in dove grey Armani. His hawk-like nose and piercing dark eyes gave him the appearance of a raptor whose hunting skills were honed over years of taking down his prey. Behind him stood another man; shorter than the first. Stockier than his companion, his ferret face had a smile that didn't quite reach his beady eyes.

"Gentlemen, how good to see you again. Can I offer you a drink?"

"No, thank you. Let's get down to business, shall we?"

"Certainly. Take a seat." Thomas moved to his desk and sat in his chair.

The two men sat in the visitors' chairs across the desk from him. "I've been hearing distressing news coming out of the Bancroft camp. Care to elaborate?"

"Now, Mr. Carter, I'm sure they are rumors. There's no need for worry."

"Really?"

"I will be seeing Mrs. Bancroft this weekend and will have it all straightened out by the beginning of next week."

"That property is prime land for me. I would hate to lose it. My sources tell me the forest is already part of a land conservancy and she has applied to have the rest made into a sanctuary for animals. I spoke to her six months ago, but as you know, she refused to sell. Since then, I've sent Harry to persuade her, but my subtle hints do not seem to have registered. She's not gone to the police with any of the 'accidents. I doubt she suspects what we've been doing. I have invested quite a lot of money into this project, including your advance of $100,000. I came today to find out what you have planned."

"As mentioned, I will be seeing her this weekend and will try to persuade her once more to sell. Andrew is on board and will also be talking to his mother."

"That buffoon. He came to see me a few months ago, all puffed up with his grand scheme. He has no idea who he's dealing with, but if he can persuade his mother to sell, I'll ignore his stupidity."

"Yes, he's an idiot, but a useful one. Don't worry. I'll handle everything this weekend."

"See that you do. I look forward to hearing from you next week." The men stood and shook hands, and the two developers left the office.

Now what could Thomas do? This had been such a great gig. Ever since inheriting Martha as a client, Thomas had been playing her. He had routinely been able to skim little bits here and there from the estate. Enough to support his addiction and keep it quite separate from his other life. She had trusted him because of his father. She never questioned his dealings with her. He prided himself on the careful and meticulous plan devised to keep his public mask in place, while living a vastly different life in private. Ruined. If Marjorie ever found out. No one must know of his room at the casino. His little oasis, he called it. His escape from the mundane life he lived with Marjorie and the kids. God, how he hated that life and everything in it. But now? After the debacle of six months ago, the whole facade could crumble like coarse meal on a baker's table. Come hell or high water, he needed to fix this and fix it now. Shit. He wished he'd never climbed into bed with Carter. That had been a huge mistake. One of many he regretted over this last year.

He remembered his conversation with Martha before the meeting Friday night. He had met her as she came down the staircase and escorted her to the library.

"I presume the conversation after dinner was somewhat anticipatory?" she said.

"Yes, ma'am. They were all wondering why you had called them here tonight."

"I suppose they badgered you to tell them."

"Yes, but I invoked my client/attorney privilege and said nothing."

Martha chuckled. "That must have put a burr under their saddles. I suppose it was Drew prodding you the most?"

"Yes, he was quite insistent that as the only remaining male and heir, it was his right to know what was going on. He tried to impress on me that you were getting on in age and were becoming frail. He suggested that it was time for him to take over the reins of the family fortune and give you a rest. I assured him that you were of very sound mind and could manage fine. He was put out but said no more."

"Arrgh," Martha responded. "I will never understand how a son of ours could turn out to be such a pompous ass. His older brother was kind-hearted and generous, but Drew resented him."

"As they say, 'we don't get to choose our families'," Tom chuckled. "But Andrew has approached me with a plan for the estate."

"Oh, has he now. I know he's got big plans for the company and the property, but I didn't know he approached you."

"Yes. I understand you have your heart set on designing a sanctuary and working farm, but I was wondering if you really feel it is best for the property. His idea of keeping the house and a few acres for the family and selling the rest might be a better wager." Martha started to object but Tom raised his hand and said, "Hear me out. He has some good points. You're not getting any younger and the scope of your dream will prove to be too much. I'm concerned that it may put a strain on your health and give you headaches you don't want. Why not sell at least part of it off and use the money to enjoy the time you have left? You could travel and visit friends. Get out of the cold in the winter. Six months in the summer here and six months in the winter wherever it's warm. You've been working hard all your life. Maybe it's time to slow down and rest."

"What on earth has gotten into you, Tom? I've no interest at all in traveling or visiting with friends. All my friends are here. Nor do I have any plans to 'slow down and rest' as you put it. I'd be bored within three days. No, this is what I want for the ranch, and I'll not be deterred. If I didn't know better, I'd swear those developers had gotten to you."

"No, no. I've never talked to them. Andrew's the one that's been doing the dealing. As I said, he made some good points and I wanted to be sure that you don't think it would be better to sell now while the prices are up."

"Sell. No thank you!"

"Think about it before you sign the will or do anything that can't be undone."

He had not convinced her to change her mind and now she was dead. What had happened to the will? No one had seen it since she died. That stupid Adele and Percy had visited and were demanding answers. As if he could answer them. Of course, it would be a lot better if it were never found, but still it was out there somewhere. They obviously didn't

121

have it, but if anyone else knew where it was it could come back to bite him in the butt. He was in deep shit this time and had to figure out what he was going to do.

Chapter Twenty-Nine

Mac sat leaning back, feet on the desk, lost in thought. It had been over two weeks since the autopsy and he still didn't have any definitive results. They'd done some digging into everyone's background, but there wasn't a lot he could do until he knew for certain it was homicide. His fingers drummed on the coffee cup held in his hands. Taking a gulp, he sat up abruptly, choking and splattering the contents onto his pants and desk.

"Shit. Who the hell made this crap?"

Joe laughed. "What's the matter? Poor baby burn his mowffie?"

"Shut up, Joe. Let's get back to the case."

Before they could begin, there was knock on the door and Cissy poked her head in.

"Ok to enter guys?"

Mac jumped up from his seat, a tiny fissure of pleasure erupting at the sight of her.

"Hey Doc. What brings you in this direction?"

"Got the toxicology reports on Mrs. Bancroft's blood and tissue samples."

"Great. What did they find?"

"Cause of death was high levels of Ketamine mixed with alcohol in her system."

"Ketamine?"

"Yes."

"Murder, then."

"Yup."

"I'd like to work with you closely on this one, Mac. Murder bums me out, but when you have a healthy woman who was sharp, decisive and a humanitarian stopped in the middle of creating a special place, it makes my blood boil."

"I hear ya. We're gonna go over what we've got. Have a chair."

Mac pulled out a chair and Cissy sat down. He and Joe approached the suspect board and looked at the rogue's gallery. Pointing to the first picture, Joe filled Mac in on what he'd learned.

"Andrew Bancroft. Fifty-three. Royally pissed about the changes in the will. Stormed out of the house but came back after talking to his wife. Said he went to his room and didn't see his wife. Was asleep when she came to their room. Has big plans for the estate. Been talking to developers. Thinks his mother's plan is a lot of garbage. Snob. Loves to party with all the 'right' people. Claims he needs more money to keep up the family image. He and his mother were estranged because of his marriage to Vanessa, so there's certainly motive there."

Mac wrote the details on the board beside Andrew's photo. "Find out if anyone saw him after he and his wife came back. This is the second Mrs. Bancroft, isn't it? Check around at the office. See if there's a third one in the wings. Talk to some of the employees. We'll need to know where he was in any negotiations with the builders and if he's dug himself into a hole because of them."

"Vanessa Bancroft. Thirty-five. Second wife of Andrew. Maiden name Waters. They were lovers before the marriage and old Mrs. Bancroft did not take kindly to the divorce and re-marriage. Vanessa had been a waitress at Woodbine where Andrew met her. Seems to be a little scatterbrained, but that could be an act. She made the hot toddy and delivered it to her mother-in-law. Maybe she didn't like being done out of the family fortune. Thought marrying Andrew was her ticket to the big time."

"Let's check on her background. Talk to old neighbors and friends. Find out if she really is simple and what they think of her. See if her mom's still alive and if she comes to visit now she's moved uptown."

"Adele Bancroft, formerly Adele Franklin. Fifty-six years old. A year older than her husband Edward. Was a secretary at Gateway when Edward was an EVP there. Said to be quite a looker in her day. Caught his eye and wham, bam, thank you ma'am, she's got him hooked. Quite a coup to catch the son and heir of the firm. According to Jared's statement, both she and Percy were enraged over the new will. Talked to her bridge buddies and they say she's a nasty piece of work. Always bragging about her trips. Loves to name drop and looks down on anyone who's different. Has only the one son, Percy. She dotes on him. Edward didn't agree with her method of child rearing, and they got into pretty heated arguments about it. He died in a plane crash. Good thing, or she probably would have been a suspect if it had been a suspicious death. Of course, to tell it now, Edward was her soul mate and she's never gotten over his death. That's why she never remarried. Bullshit. She wanted to keep Percy to herself and enjoy her social status. That's the only thing that matters to her.

"Let's keep a close eye on her."

Percy Bancroft. Thirty-four years old. Little creep. Hates his grandmother and his cousin. Dr. Bancroft was favored over him and that really rankles. Thinks he's the next great composer. Supposed to be studying music. Ran a check on his teacher, 'The Maestro'. Two-bit con artist has struck it big with his latest scheme. Got a bunch of wealthy artsy fartsy types under his thumb. Spend all their time in cafes, art museums and music halls discussing who knows what. All convinced by the Maestro they are the next great Mozart and need a chance to be discovered. Really got a hold on Percy. Spoke to a couple of the 'friends. Supposed to go on some trip to Europe in the summer to, as they put it, 'broaden their musical horizons by walking in the footsteps of the great Masters'. Stupid asses. Anyway, Percy was livid with his grandmother for not supporting his grand adventure."

"Do more digging into this Maestro guy. Seems like he'd have motive. If Percy's cut off, so is he. Look harder at Percy. See what, if anything, he knows about Ketamine. Find out his financials and see what else his gang of punks are up to."

"Jared Bancroft. Thirty-three. Veterinarian, although Dad, Andrew,

125

is not impressed. Not classy enough for him. Only one of the group who appeared to genuinely love his grandmother. Talk is, they were close. With the new will, he does get an advantage. He will oversee the research facility and have access to the money to run it. But you never know. Might be something underneath all that charm."

"Talk to his colleagues. See if we can find anything that would lead us to believe he'd be better off with the old will in place. Maybe he's overextended and needs ready cash. Could have other problems which need immediate funds. Let's see what we can find."

"Thomas Winslow. Forty-nine. Lawyer for the Bancroft family. Took over from his father when senior died. Seems to be okay. Lives in an upscale house near in Ashburn, but nothing he couldn't afford on his salary. Married. Couple of kids, one graduating university and another graduating high school. Wife on the board of various local charities. Seems she spends a lot of time on them. Talked to her friends. All agreed she was 'dedicated' and a 'tireless worker'. She goes to a lot of conferences and conventions for these organizations. Appears a lot of the money raised is spent sending delegates to fancy hotels and parties. Maybe she needs more money to keep her lifestyle going."

"Get a search warrant and information from the Justice of the Peace to check into all their financials and phone records. We need to have a better picture of where they all stand and who gains the most if the new will isn't found. Good start. Why don't you see what you can dig up? I'm going to take a run out to the house to see if I can find any trace of that will. Catch you later. Wanna come with me, Doc?"

"Sure. No problem."

Chapter Thirty

T he gravel crunched under the tires as the car drove through the front gates of the estate. The main house glistened in the late morning sun. Mac pulled to a stop in front of the wide steps. He and Cissy opened their doors and stepped out.

Mac stretched his arms above his head, extending his fingers and inhaling a lung full of air in the process. "Ah, wonderful fragrance of Eau de Manure. Very refreshing."

"Better than Eau de Morgue," Cissy laughed.

"Touché, dear doctor. Shall we see who's home?"

"Lead on, MacDuff."

They climbed the front steps and rang the doorbell. No one answered. They waited a few moments and rang again. All was silent. "It doesn't look like anyone's home. Let's try around the back."

Walking around the side of the house, Cissy gasped. "How beautiful. I didn't see this part when I was here the other night."

Acres of rolling hills with woodlands in the distance spread out in a wonderful tapestry of colours. Gleaming white barns surrounded by rail fences stood off to her right. Four horses, their coats shimmering in the sunlight, grazed in one of the paddocks. A frisky colt ran with his mane and tail streaming out behind as if he were a school child let out for summer vacation. Attached to the barn was a square building resembling a small house. Mac and Cissy walked downhill toward it. A sign to the right of the door read "OFFICE Jared Bancroft, DVM". Mac tried the door. It was not locked. They stepped through. About a quarter of the way into the room, a counter holding a small silver bell stood across from the entrance. Shelves filled with animal food and paraphernalia lined the walls behind the registration desk. Near the back of the room on the left wall was a door connecting to the barn. Folding chairs lined an anteroom to their right. A large scale hugged one wall of the alcove. Cissy sauntered over to the side room and peered in. This was the heart of the practice. The large examination rooms, offices and a hallway leading to surgery suites, were bright and airy, lending to an atmosphere of calm proficiency for both patient and owner.

Mac walked to the counter and dinged the bell. Within a few seconds the back door opened and a young woman holding a black cat entered the room.

"May I help you?"

"Detective Ian MacKellar and Dr. Cecilia Walsh. We are investigating the death of Mrs. Martha Bancroft. Are any family members at home?"

"I'm Charli Bancroft, Mrs. Bancroft's granddaughter. How can I help you, detective?"

"We'd like to inspect Mrs. Bancroft's room one more time. Can you let us into the house?"

"Have you talked to my dad? He wasn't happy with the whole police involvement with Grandma's death. I don't think he'd like you traipsing around the house again."

"I understand Ms. Bancroft, but there have been new developments in the situation, and I need to see Mrs. Bancroft's room once more. I can get a search warrant, but it will save us a lot of time if we can look around while we're here."

"I need to call my dad." Charli set the cat on the counter and pulled out a cell from her jeans pocket. Scurrying through the back entrance, she pulled the door closed behind her.

"So, this is Dr. Bancroft's office. Nice digs. Guess Grandma didn't spare any expense. Makes sense to have his office here since he's the vet for the ranch," remarked Mac.

"Handy source for the Ketamine."

"Right. Forgot it was a horse tranquilizer before it became a street drug. Convenient."

"Opens up the realm of opportunity."

"That it does. Wonder if there's any missing?"

The door opened and Charli came back into the room. "I've spoken with my father and to say he is not happy with you being here, is an understatement. He's on his way home and asks if you will remain until he arrives."

"We can wait. In the meantime, is it all right if we start our search?"

"I guess so. Come with me."

The threesome left the office, walked up the hill to the kitchen door and entered the house.

"Is this door usually unlocked?"

"Yes. We have regular mealtimes for all our employees, but anyone can come in to get a snack at any time. When you're in the middle of foaling or treating a sick animal, you can't always get away when the dinner gong chimes."

"What about at night?"

"Would depend on what's happening. If there's stuff going on, either Jared or I might leave the door open so that we can get to the barns quickly without fumbling for keys. We're usually staying in the house at those times."

"Was anything going on the night of your grandmother's dinner party?"

"Yes. We were watching a sick horse."

"The door would have been unlatched?"

"Yes."

"Anyone could've come in or out at anytime?"

"I suppose so."

"Thank you, Ms. Bancroft. We'll make our way to your grandmother's room now."

Mac walked through to the front of the house. Taking out his cell, he punched a speed dial number.

"Joe, I need you to get a warrant for forensics to search Dr. Bancroft's veterinary clinic at the ranch. Yeah, I want to see his last order for Ketamine and if any of it is missing. Get a check on his phone and emails as well. I'm here at the house. Had a chat with a Charlotte Bancroft, Dr. Jared's sister. The back door was left open the night of the dinner. Anyone could've tampered with the toddy. Raises some interesting questions. Ok. See ya."

Mac and Cissy walked up the staircase.

Chapter Thirty-One

Hearing voices coming from the kitchen, Martha and Gladys zoomed from the living room, where they had been discussing the investigation, to the hallway, in time to hear Mac's phone call to Joe.

"They're back!" Martha asked. "But why are they talking about Jared?"

"I wonder if they have the results of the autopsy?"

"Yes. Now we'll find out what happened to me."

"Then can we move on?"

"Depends on what they found. Let's follow them and see why they're back."

With that announcement, Martha swirled out of the room and upstairs to her old bedroom.

As Mac and Cissy were climbing the staircase, Cissy suddenly shivered.

"Did you feel that?"

"What?"

"A coldness, like being showered with a bucket of ice water."

"No, I didn't feel a thing."

"Odd. It's gone now. Wonder if it was Martha?"

"You really do believe in ghosts?"

"Let's just say I've had otherwise unexplainable experiences."

"Huh. I didn't take you for a woo-woo kind of person."

"If you mean a person who believes there's more to life than what we can see or touch, then ya, you could say that. But then you don't know me very well."

"I know this isn't the time, but I'd like to remedy that situation. Would you have dinner with me one night?"

"That's the weirdest pickup line I've ever heard. If you're serious, I'd love to talk about ghosts, ghoulies and things that go bump in the night," laughed Cissy wiggling her eyebrows. "Instead of dinner, why don't we make it lunch at Have a Cuppa in Port Perry. I'd like to include Becca if you don't mind."

"Sure, but why Becca?"

"I told you she and I had a very strange experience a couple of years ago. She promised she'll tell you about it if you are interested. It might help you understand what's been going on here."

"You really think Martha's still here, don't you?"

"Yup, I do. If she helps us find the will, what are you afraid of?"

"I'm not afraid of anything. Ok. You're on. If we don't find anything today, you set up a time with Becca and I'll listen. Not saying I'll believe her, but at least I should hear a good story."

Chapter Thirty-Two

The shrouded bedroom smelled musty as Mac opened the door. The duo entered as Gladys joined Martha in their usual corner. Cissy flicked on the light which cast a gloomy pall over the furnishings.

"Where do you want to start?"

Mac shoved his hands through his hair. "The will wasn't signed when she left the meeting the other night, but she did tell her lawyer she wanted to review it. He gave it to her in a manila envelope. She had it when she went to bed. What happened to it after that, no one seems to know. Winslow claims he doesn't have it. If it isn't here, somebody's lying, but who?"

"Maybe she had a secret nook in here? Or a safe?"

"If there is a safe, nobody appears to know about it. Must be hidden well. Look for anything that's out of alignment or a hollow wall."

Mac and Cissy looked behind the books on the bookcase, in the closets and tapped the walls and floors. They lifted down the paintings, mirrors and looked under the bed. Martha watched as they methodically made a futile search.

"Over here," Martha shouted in exasperation. "I need to get them to come closer to the fireplace." She focussed on a pottery horse figurine on the left side of the mantle. Concentrating all her energy onto the object, the statue started to rock, then sway and finally came crashing down onto the hearth, breaking into shards.

Both investigators jumped in reaction.

"What the hell was that?" shouted Mac.

"The horse on the mantle fell and smashed onto the hearth."

"How?"

"Dunno. One minute it was standing there, the next, it shattered

133

when it hit the floor," said Cissy. Mac took a sideways glance at Cissy, his hands shaking. He noticed she was pale and was rubbing her arms. *Not as cool about ghosts as she thinks she is.*

Martha gasped. "Get over here. I am trying to show you where the safe is."

"Good call. That brought them in a hurry," snorted Gladys.

"Shut up and let me think. Maybe if I wiggle the pieces around, they'll come over." She concentrated again on the broken shards of pottery making them rattle on the cold stone.

Mac's heart rose into his throat. "Umm... guess it's time to go."

He and Cissy exited the room and closed the door. "Set up the lunch with Rebecca and we'll see what she has to say. I'm getting desperate. Don't say anything to Joe. He'd eat me alive if he knew we were talking about ghost stuff."

Her eyes twinkling, Cissy responded. "Don't tell me the big tough policeman is embarrassed. Don't worry. Not my place to share. That's your call."

"Thanks."

Mac and Cissy walked down the stairs as the front door opened and Andrew rushed through. Both parties came to an abrupt halt.

"There you are, Detective. Why are you here again?"

"I'm sorry, Mr. Bancroft, but as I mentioned to your daughter, there have been new developments. I have received the official coroner's report and death was due to poisoning. This is now a homicide investigation."

Shock coursed through Martha's energy field. "Poisoned! Murdered? That's why I felt funny after drinking the toddy. That phone call sounded like Mac suspects Jared."

"Well, now you know how you died. We can move on."

"Not on your life. I need to figure out who killed me. I will not let my grandson be blamed for a murder he didn't do."

"Oh, good grief! There's nothing you can do. You're sure he didn't do it?"

"Yes, I'm sure. Damn. I was about to start my dream and one of these idiots has taken it away. I'm going to make his or her life miserable."

"Not a good idea. You might get stuck here."

"I don't care. How dare they? It was my life. They had no right!" Small sparks like a sparkler at a fireworks display emanated from Martha's light ball. The light disappeared from the corner and Gladys raced after it.

"Homicide? There must be a mistake," huffed Andrew. "The funeral was only a couple of weeks ago and we are just starting to move on from the tremendous shock. Now you're opening everything up again. I want to speak to the coroner."

"That's no problem at all. Dr. Cecilia Walsh, Forensic Pathologist, Mr. Andrew Bancroft, son of the deceased," Mac introduced them.

Andrew took one look at Cissy and frowned. "Now, see here young lady, I don't know who you are, but I suspect your competency, if that's the conclusion you drew from your post-mortem. My Mother died of a heart attack. That's all. We should talk to your supervisor. I'm sure he will help you see you made a mistake, and the death was from natural causes. No need to be embarrassed. We all make mistakes from time to time. Let's have a drink and talk it over."

Cissy smiled at Andrew, her blood pressure rising. She looked him straight in the eye. "How do you do, Mr. Bancroft. Thank you for your invitation, but I can assure you there is no need to discuss anything. I am quite positive of my findings, and the results have been given to the police. Mrs. Bancroft did indeed die from poison. The autopsy results will not be changed."

Andrew spluttered, little bubbles of spittle appearing at the corners of his mouth. "My dear young woman. I am a man of importance in this town. I will speak to the Chief Coroner and the Chief of Police about this matter. I never wanted an autopsy in the first place and now you are making a preposterous claim that my mother was murdered."

"I am aware of the Bancroft name, sir. That is why I ordered an autopsy. You are free to call whomever you wish, but it will not alter the findings."

"We'll see about that," said Andrew, his face burning red, hands tightly fisted at his side.

Mac stepped between the dueling pair. "Mr. Bancroft, I would like you to call all the dinner guests from the party and ask them to meet here tonight at eight o'clock. I will inform them of the nature of your mother's death and will have further questions for each of you."

"That's outrageous. You can't expect me to get everyone together on such short notice."

"Oh, but I do, and you will advise them that it will be in their best interests to cooperate fully."

Chapter Thirty-Three

In the time between Mac's conversation with Andrew and the meeting, Gladys found Martha and managed to calm her down. Convincing her they needed to hear the discussion, Martha and Gladys glided into the room and took up their usual positions by the curtain. At eight o'clock, Mac stood inside the doorway of the living room. Gazing at the tableau in front of him, he was reminded of a set from an Agatha Christie movie. The lord of the manor stood erect behind a wing chair in which sat his lady. The widowed aunt and her son were on the couch; she, holding a handkerchief and dabbing her eyes. The grandson and heir stood at the window looking out over the landscape and the lawyer sat at a lady's desk with an open briefcase in front of him. Mac shook his head to clear the illusion of a play from his mind and walked to the center of the room.

"Thank you all for coming. I'm sure by now that Mr. Bancroft has informed you of the results of the toxicology done on Mrs. Martha Bancroft. Unfortunately, those results showed she did not die of natural causes."

"Preposterous," stated Andrew.

"No sir. The tests were quite conclusive." Mac paused. Putting on a solemn mask, his eyes piercing Andrew with a glance, he said, "Of course, you could have the body exhumed and an independent lab of your choosing could do their own tests."

"What? Exhume my mother! Absolutely not!"

"I thought not," Mac replied.

"If, as you say, she did not die of natural causes, what killed her? You mentioned poison to me earlier. If that's correct what's it called? Perhaps it was an accidental overdose of one of her prescription meds."

"No sir. This was no accident. A large quantity of Ketamine was

137

found in her system."

"Ketamine?" remarked Jared, startled.

All eyes in the room turned to where Jared was standing.

"Yes, Dr. Bancroft. You recognize it?"

"Of course. I use it in my practice. It is a general anesthetic used in veterinary medicine."

"True."

Martha and Gladys both gasped.

"That's why he suspects Jared."

"Appears so," Gladys responded. "But it has nothing to do with us now."

"Maybe not to you, but it certainly does to me."

"I still don't see what we can do."

"I don't either, but I'll figure it out."

Mac continued. "This home is now a crime scene. Mrs. Bancroft's bedroom will be cordoned off and no one will be permitted to go in. Your lab has been cleared, Dr. Bancroft as the forensic team was here earlier."

"Most of us are staying at the house until the estate is settled," snapped Andrew. "I presume it's alright with you."

"Yes. You can stay here, but don't go into her room and don't leave town without letting me know."

Percy raised his hand and signaled Mac. "I say, old boy, I was planning a trip to the Maestro's cottage in Muskoka next weekend. I really can't miss this rare opportunity to spend quality time with him. What shall I do?"

Mac's eyes flickered in distaste for a millisecond as he turned to face Percy. "If you will give us an address and phone number where we can reach you, I'm sure we can work something out, Mr. Bancroft."

"Oh, thank heavens. I must say I would be rather distraught to miss this chance." He leaned back into the sofa and took his mother's hand. Adele smiled at her son and patted his hand gently.

"Does anyone have anything else to say?"

Vanessa turned to Andrew. "Andy," she whispered. "I need to talk to you."

"Not now Vanessa. This is not the time. We have a crisis on our hands, and I have to think."

"But, Andy, it's important."

"Not now, I said. Oh, go look after Zeus or something. Don't bother me."

"Do you want to speak, Mrs. Bancroft?" asked Mac.

"No, I... no."

"Alright. You can all go about your business, but I will need to interview you all again. Please be ready when I call you in."

Mac and Joe left the room and exited the house.

"Well, this is a fine turn of events. Murdered. Who would want to murder Mother? Thomas join me in the library. We need to talk," said Andrew. He turned and left the room. Thomas put his papers back in the briefcase, picked it up and followed Andrew.

"Percy, dear, please escort me to my room. I'm afraid I shan't sleep a wink tonight knowing there's a killer on the loose. I'll need my medicine as well. My heart can't take this kind of strain."

"It's all right, Mother. I'll take care of you." Percy stood and helped his mother to stand. Leaning on her son, the two left the room.

"I guess that leaves us," said Jared. "What did you want to tell my dad?"

Vanessa looked at her stepson, tears in pools on her lower eyelids. "Nothing important. It can wait. I'd better go and look after Zeus. He's missing his Mommy." Hands shaking, she lifted them to her eyes to wipe away the moisture. Rising from the chair, she scurried across the rug and out the door.

Ketamine. I need to check my supply. Jared turned from the window, went through the kitchen and out the back door to his office. All was silent in the living room. The two orbs became brighter and morphed into human figures.

139

"They all know now. Mac definitely suspects Jared, but my grandson has no reason to kill me."

"Well, we don't know that. Let's follow him and see what he's going to do next."

Chapter Thirty-Four

The night was overcast as Jared hurried down to his clinic. The way was so familiar, he needed no light to guide him. Martha and Gladys followed. Stunned by the revelation Ketamine killed his grandmother, his mind was in a fog. Why would a murderer use that particular poison unless they wanted to implicate him? But who? He knew his dad was talking to developers and wanted to sell the property for housing, but to kill his own mother and implicate his son? No. He couldn't do that, could he? Then there was Adele and Percy. They hated him but would they really plot to get both he and his grandmother out of the way? Who else could it be? Thomas? But he had nothing to gain, did he?

He stumbled into his clinic and turned on the light. He hadn't taken two steps forward when the door to the barn opened and Charli stepped through.

"I saw the light go on. Figured it was you. What did the police want?"

"You're not going to believe it. He said that Grandma was murdered."

"What!"

"Yeah."

"But how?"

"That's the worst part. By an overdose of Ketamine."

"Ketamine?"

"Yup."

"Who would do such a thing? How would they know how to use it?"

"I don't know, but it looks like someone is trying to set me up. I've got to check my supply."

141

⟡

As Jared moved past Charli, Martha and Gladys slid into his surgery and hid high on a shelf. He opened his supply cabinet and searched through his stock of medicine.

"I had a new supply sent a couple of weeks ago." A chill moved through his body. He rummaged in the cupboard, pulling out bottles, vials, bandages, and other objects used in his day-to-day routines. "Charli, the bottle I opened for Grace's surgery is gone. The Forensic Team must have taken it when they were here. It was almost full as I only used the 10-ccs required for the operation. What if more had been taken out of the bottle?"

"I don't like the sound of that," said Martha.

"Oh, Jared. This is terrible. What are you going to do?"

"I don't know, but I didn't kill her. I loved her. Charli."

"Of course, he didn't kill me," Martha huffed.

"You don't know that," replied Gladys.

"I do know that. What motive could he have?"

"I don't know, but there could be one."

"That detective can't possibly think you had anything to do with it. You loved her and besides, you had nothing to gain," said Charli.

"I… I guess not."

"What aren't you telling me?"

"Well, there's Kelly."

"What do you mean, 'there's Kelly'? Who's she?"

"You remember when I went to Whistler last year?"

"Yes."

"Well, I met someone. Her name is Kelly, and she was one of the girls who cleaned my cabin every day. We got talking and—"

"And?"

"I've been seeing her ever since. She's special and I love her. It's taken a bit of time, but she's moving here to be with me."

"And you haven't told anyone? What aren't you saying? Why would

142

she be a problem anyway?"

"I did talk to Mom, and she agreed I shouldn't tell Grandma until everything was settled. Also, Kelly has a little girl, whom I plan to adopt so there's an added wrinkle."

"Why didn't you tell me? I wouldn't say anything."

"I wanted to, but Mom and I figured the fewer people who knew, the better. In Grandma's eyes, it would be Aunt Adele and Vanessa all over again. A cleaning woman. Good Lord! She'd have a fit. As if it wasn't a respectable job. Kelly isn't like them, but Grandma wouldn't know that. You know how she could be. I could even picture her giving me an ultimatum. Either give up Kelly or lose the ranch. I wanted to ease Grandma into it. I love this ranch. Grandma's plans are the kind of work I've always wanted to do, Charli. I couldn't risk it. What if MacKellar found out about Kelly and thinks I have a motive?"

"Oh, my lord... that's horrible," exclaimed Martha. "Why would Jared think I would reject anyone he loved?"

"Your track record isn't the greatest," answered Gladys.

Martha paused. "Even so, I didn't cut off Ed or Drew for their poor choices. Why would he think I'd make him choose between his love and his job?"

"You were pretty vocal about your dislike of Adele and Vanessa. Maybe he thought you'd be so fed up with another 'unsuitable' love interest, you'd fire him. I don't know, but he obviously felt you wouldn't approve. More important, if the detective's thinking along those lines, he'll think it gives him motive to kill you before you could fire him. Let's hear what they're saying now."

"Pretty weak motive for murder, if you ask me," said Charli.

"Yeah, well, it's not your drug, is it?"

"Don't be ridiculous. Anyone could have come in here and taken some out of the bottle. The cupboard and the office are locked when we're not here, sure, but the whole family knows the cupboard keys are in your drawer and the front door lock wouldn't be hard to open for a determined killer. C'mon. Let's go back to the house. There's nothing more we can do tonight. Talk to the detective. He'll figure it out."

Charli took her brother's arm and led him out of the clinic, turning off the lights as they went.

The following morning, Mac and Joe were in their office discussing the case.

"Ok, Joe. What's the latest?"

"We've checked into Bancroft Senior's financials', and everything seems on the up and up there. He did have a meeting with the developers a while back and appeared to be talking with Winslow as well. My assumption is he wanted to sell, but his mother squelched it. By all accounts he was terribly angry with the arrangements outlined at the meeting. Would give him ample motive to kill his mother. Checked into Bancroft Junior. He's respected by the animal community around here. He and his sister are well liked and have worked hard with their grandmother to build her dream. One interesting piece of info I picked up is that he's having an affair with a woman he met last year at a resort. She was his cleaning lady. Has a little girl. No father in the picture. Maybe the old lady got wind of the situation and blew her top. It would be like her sons' marriages, only in the next generation. Other than that, neither he nor his sister seem to have a motive. From the gossip, they really did love Mrs. Bancroft. They're the ones most hurt if the new will isn't found, so I can't see them withholding it. As far as the Ketamine is concerned, the forensic guys checked out his clinic and the surrounding area. They did find a partially opened bottle of it in a locked cupboard which they bagged. The night of the party, Dr. Bancroft was treating a sick horse. That could explain why it was opened. Unfortunately, for him, the only fingerprints on the bottle were his."

"Let's bring him in and see if he can explain what happened."

"Got it. Next, Mrs. Adele Bancroft and her son Percy. He certainly wouldn't like being shut out of his family's fortune. Not finding the will would be helpful for him and his mother. She grew up in a lower middle-class home. Her dad was a mechanic, and her mom was a stay-at-home with six kids. Quite a looker back in the day and managed to land a job as her late husband's secretary. It appears she's gotten very used to being a lady of leisure and likes it that way. Losing her inheritance would put a crimp in her activities. That give us motive. Don't know if she knows anything about Ketamine though. I need to do a little more digging. Sid, in drugs, brought in a snitch. He tipped me off 'cause the guy seems to know Percy's little group. Could be nothing, but you never know. I'm going to sit in on the interview after we're finished here. I'll let you know what he says."

As Joe was updating Mac on his part of the investigation, the phone rang.

"Detective MacKellar."

"Detective, this is Jared Bancroft. I want to inform you I have gone over my inventory of Ketamine. We had a sick horse the night of my grandmother's party and I opened a new bottle to use, but when I checked my stock last night, the bottle was gone. I presume you have it?"

"Yes, Doctor. I have it. Could you come into the office? I have a few more questions for you."

"Of course, Detective. When would it be convenient for you?"

"Now would be good."

He heard Jared sigh over the phone. "Alright. I'll leave now. I should be there in about twenty minutes."

Mac hung up the phone. "Interesting. He's coming in. Said it should take him about twenty minutes. Could be he's guilty or being set up. Either way, let's put a little pressure on."

Chapter Thirty-Five

Martha and Gladys listened to the phone call. Jared turned to Charli as he clicked off his cell and replaced it in his pocket. "What did he say?"

"He wants me to come in for further questioning."

"You did not kill Grandma!"

"Thanks for believing me, Sis, but I'm not sure the Detective does."

"You'd best get down there and convince him of the truth."

"I will. Hold the fort, okay?"

"Sure."

"Let's go with him to hear what the detective has to say," said Martha.

"Okey dokey," replied Gladys.

Jared left the clinic and walked to his car accompanied by the two spirits. He took his time driving into town and to the police building. Entering the precinct, he saw a glass partition behind which three police officers manned a desk. He walked up to the first window. An officer approached him.

"Can I help you?"

"I'm here to see Detective MacKellar. My name is Jared Bancroft."

"Hold on. I call him." The officer picked up the phone. "Mac, there's a Jared Bancroft here to see you." She turned to Jared and told him, "Take a seat. He'll be with you shortly."

After waiting twenty minutes, the inner door opened, and Mac stepped into the waiting room. "Thanks for coming in Dr. Bancroft. Please follow me." Mac led him through the door and down the hallway to an interrogation room.

"It's about time. Wouldn't have kept me waiting that long, I tell ya. Trying to make him sweat," huffed Martha.

"Please take a seat."

Jared took a seat at the table in the center of the room. Mac sat opposite him and laid a folder on the surface. Jared handed Mac the invoice for the Ketamine. Mac picked up the paper and said, "Dr. Bancroft, this is the order for the medication. Is that correct?"

"Yes."

"I see you ordered two bottles of Ketamine. Correct?"

"Yes."

"What happened to those bottles?"

"I locked them in my medicine cabinet at the clinic. We're careful with any meds we have for our practice."

"What happened to them?" asked Mac.

"I opened one bottle for the surgery I mentioned to you. The weight of the animal is used to calculate the dosage. With Grace, we used ten ccs. The bottle was then put back in the cabinet with the unopened one. When you mentioned Ketamine as the poison which killed my grandmother, I checked my supply. The opened bottle was missing."

"Is this the bottle?" said Mac as he showed him a bottle containing a liquid.

"It appears to be."

"After using it in the surgery, you replaced it in the cupboard?"

"I did."

"Did anyone else handle the bottle?"

"Not that I'm aware of."

"You told me that you only used ten ccs of the drug, but this bottle is only three quarters full. There's a lot more than ten ccs missing. What do you suppose happened to the rest?"

"I don't know."

"You locked the cabinet when you finished the surgery?"

"Yes."

"Was the lock forced?"

"No."

"Who has keys?"

"They are kept in a box in my desk drawer."

"Who has knowledge of where they're kept?"

"The family."

"So, anyone in the family could have taken them from your drawer and opened the cabinet?"

"Correct. But the door to the office is always locked when Charli and I aren't there."

"Do you have anything else you'd like to add?"

"No. I've told you everything I know."

"Really? Well, that will be all for now, Dr. Bancroft. Please keep yourself available for further questioning, should we need it."

"I didn't do it, I tell you. I loved my grandmother. I would never hurt her. You must believe me."

"Thank you, Doctor. You're free to go. I'm sure you can find your way out."

"Uh-oh. Not looking good for the boy," whispered Gladys.

"He didn't do it. We have to convince Mac of that," replied Martha. "Let's get back to the house and see what we can figure out."

Chapter Thirty-Six

M ac picked up his file and walked back to his office. After studying the contents, he walked over to the suspect board and wrote on it. As he added the new information, the door opened, and Joe walked in.

"How'd the interview go?" he asked.

"He brought in the invoice and the code on the bottle matches the info on the order. They're definitely his. Doesn't tell us who used the contents. Didn't tell me about his situation with his girlfriend. I'm wondering why not. What's he hiding? I was going over the timeline to see if anything jumps out. We know the drug was in the hot toddy and it sat on the kitchen table for at least five minutes unattended. At that point, Jared, Adele, and later Percy were in the library, so they say. Andrew says he was in his room as does Thomas. Vanessa left the kitchen to attend to a noise in the pantry. Charli could have come in from the barn, seen the toddy and slipped in the poison, but that doesn't seem likely. I've interviewed all the ranch hands and there's nothing there."

"Yeah, and it doesn't appear Jared could have done it as he and Adele alibi each other. Since they hate each other's guts, it seems unlikely they would vouch for one another. Appears he's been set up, but by who? Although Adele was already in the library when he got there, and Percy didn't arrive until much later. Andrew and Thomas didn't want the will signed. From everything I can gather, they were in cahoots with the developers. I did find out there were incidents at the ranch starting about six months ago."

"Oh, what happened?" asked Mac.

"Fire in one of the barns. One of the hands came back unexpectedly and put it out. A few weeks later, Jared found part of their boundary

149

fence down. Animals could have escaped. Then Mrs. Bancroft had a narrow escape with a large truck tire which almost hit her but didn't. Could be coincidence, but the developers showed up at a big fundraiser the old lady was having for her sanctuary and there was a row. Several people overheard her tell them the only way they were going to get her property was over her dead body."

"Interesting. What do we know about these guys?"

"Fairly new on the scene but got a couple of high-priced contracts. Scuttlebutt is that they're on the edge when it comes to regulations and the environment. They've been trying to get approval to build on the Moraine, but so far have been held off. If they could get the Bancroft estate, it would be a big coup and puts them that much closer to opening up the greenbelt for construction."

"Keep poking that particular horse. Find out what Andrew and Thomas have to do with them and how closely they're tied. If either of those two owe them, that's motive for murder."

"Will do. I came to tell you that I sat in on the interview with the drug dealer."

"And?"

"He knows Percy all right. He and his buddies are regular customers of his. He did sell him a small amount of Special 'K' a couple of weeks ago. That gives him means. He would know what the drug could do. Hatred for his grandmother and cousin gives him a good motive for nixing her and trying to blame the good doctor."

"According to the toxicology report the drug used came from Dr. Bancroft's stock. Interesting tidbit but doesn't help us much."

"No, but we do know he knew about it and what it could do."

"True. Let's keep an eye on him."

"Sure. What about the attempt on Dr. Walsh?"

"Spur of the moment. Probably when our perp first heard about the autopsy."

"How so?"

"Impulsive. Smacks of rage. The poison was cold and deliberate.

150

The truck attack wasn't."

"I see what you mean. Well, I'll keep digging into the money angle."

"Great. I'm done for the day. I'll be at home if you need me. Call as soon as you get the info."

Chapter Thirty-Seven

The golden sunrise was peeking over the horizon as Mac sauntered onto his back deck, coffee in hand. Leaning on the railing, he mulled over the case. Martha Bancroft had been a stalwart in the community for as long as he could remember. The estate produced champion thoroughbreds and he enjoyed watching them frolic in the fields whenever he'd chance to pass by. He thought about the autopsy results. Murder. Running his fingers through his hair, he thought about the complications of not finding a signed will. As things stood, Andrew and Adele were the beneficiaries under the old one. They would sell to the developers. Ugh. More square box houses. More tiny yards and winding streets. More people. Unfortunately, he and Cissy found nothing when they searched the house. Weird, though. The horse crashing on the tile when no one was near it. Ghosts. A tiny shiver went through him. What if Martha was still around? Both Cissy and her friend Rebecca thought it possible. Shit. He liked Cissy. With her warm laugh and grey eyes that changed color with her moods, he was hoping to get to know her a lot better. But ghosts? Could he accept that? Dunno. Kinda creeps me out. His cell rang.

"Mac, it's Cissy. I've talked to Becca. Do you have time to meet us at the tea house in Port Perry? I think you'll find her story interesting."

"I don't know, Cissy. I'm not comfortable with talking about ghosts."

"I know but hear her out. It might help with the search for the will."

"Well, I could use help with that. Forensics has been all over the room; I'm sure the family's been snooping around, and we've looked a couple of times. The only other explanation is that Winslow has it. If he has, why hasn't he come forward with it? Unless he's holding it ransom from Bancroft Sr. It sure would help to find it.

"Then come to Port. Becca's willing to help and at this point, it's worth a shot."

"Alright. It'll take me about twenty minutes to get there."

"We'll be waiting."

The bell over the door of "Have a Cuppa" jangled, signaling a customer was entering the cafe. Cissy looked up from the corner booth at the back of the room.

"Here he is."

She got up from her seat and walked to the front. Grabbing Mac's hand, she led him back to the booth. "We've ordered. What would you like?"

"A cup of java would be great."

Cissy called the waitress to their table and Mac placed his order. As the waitress left, Mac turned to Rebecca.

"I don't know what Cissy has told you, Rebecca, but I don't believe in ghosts so you're wasting your time."

"I hear you. I was as skeptical as you, two years ago. Everything about ghosts or the supernatural made me extremely uncomfortable. Then came my experience and I could no longer deny their existence. I'll share what happened and you can take it from there. Three years ago, my dad died, and it sent me into a tailspin. I started having panic attacks and was sick for months with my family hovering over me. I couldn't stand it. As soon as possible, I took a drive around the Port Perry area looking for a place of my own. A sanctuary, if you will, where I could hide from my family, lick my wounds, and heal in peace. I found Stone Cottage. The sensation of coming home flooded my heart, although I'd never seen the place before. It was for sale, so I grabbed it. It felt right until I met the resident ghost. Her name was Victoria Anne McBride, but her friends called her Annie. Even more than seeing the human ghost, she had a dog spirit with her. That really shook me up. I

153

learned his name was Thor and he'd stayed around to protect her. She'd been an earthbound entity for over one hundred and fifty years. The first time I saw them, it scared the life out of me, and I ran out of the house. My whole body was shaking. When I calmed down enough to drive, I went straight home and had Cissy meet me there. She has more experience than I do with these things."

"Come into my parlor said the spider to the fly," Cissy whispered in her best Draculin voice.

They all laughed.

"The dog is the Thor of 'Thor's Sanctuary'?"

"Yes. I wanted to honor his love and loyalty for Annie. What better way than to have a place for wounded and lost dogs to recover and find their forever homes. We did a lot of research on the property and the people involved. Mr. William McBride built the house for his bride, Annie. I did find out why she appeared to me and no one else. We were also able to find a connection between the two of us. The whole experience was overwhelming but after the encounters, I could no longer deny that ghosts do exist. I haven't had any more incidents like it. Cissy mentioned there may be a ghost involved in this case, although how I can help, I don't know."

"Thanks, Rebecca. I've had a couple of experiences at the Bancroft estate since the night of the murder and I'm not sure what to make of them. It sounds ridiculous, but I'm beginning to wonder if Martha is still around and trying to help me somehow."

Mac proceeded to tell Rebecca about the weird things that happened at the house. "Cissy was with me the last time. She can affirm that no one was near the horse when it fell. Spooked me. I couldn't get out of the room fast enough."

"Same as me when I first saw Annie and Thor."

"I didn't see anyone, just the horse falling."

"If you'd like, we could all go to the house, and I'll see if I can sense anything. I'm not a psychic or a medium or anything like that. Annie was my first and only experience with a ghost. Maybe it was a unique situation, and I won't be able to feel or see Martha, but we can try."

"Thanks. I'd appreciate it. I don't want anyone to know about this. I feel stupid enough already and the guys would never let me live it down, but if Martha is there and wants to talk, I'd like to know."

"Sure thing. Let me know when you want to meet, and I'll be there."

Chapter Thirty-Eight

His cell started ringing as Mac stepped into his car.

"Hey, Joe, what's up?"

"Found something interesting in digging into Winslow's financials. You'll want to see this. Meet me at the station."

"Be right there."

Mac hung up and peeled away from the curb. Within fifteen minutes he was in the office looking at the suspect board.

"Everything looked like it should on the surface, but Maggie found an encrypted file. We hit pay dirt. Our esteemed counselor has a hidden life. The file showed he is a regular at a casino in Niagara. Even has a permanent room for his private use. Bills for upscale call girls, booze and of course, gambling. Has quite an addiction, by the looks of it. About eight months ago, he got into a spot of trouble. Everything had been going great until he lost a lot of money one weekend."

"How much are we talking?"

"A hundred grand."

"Whoa."

"Funny thing is, about a month later, the bill was paid in full. Where'd he get that kind of cash without his wife finding out?"

"We should have another little talk with our esteemed solicitor. Let's take a ride."

Mac and Joe grabbed their coats and drove to the Winslow offices. Entering the main door, they strode to the front reception desk.

"Detectives MacKellar and Surrey to see Mr. Thomas Winslow."

"I'm sorry, Detective, but Mr. Winslow hasn't come in yet this morning."

"Is he usually this late?"

"No. I've been trying to reach him, but he's not answering."

"I'll leave you my card. If he does get in touch, please let him know we're anxious to talk to him."

"Certainly."

The two detectives left the building and walked to their car. Once seated in the vehicle, Joe asked, "Where to?"

"Let's take a run out to his house."

"Sure thing."

Joe started the car and the two partners drove out to Thomas's home. As they pulled into the driveway, they noticed his car parked in front of the garage. Signaling quiet, Mac exited the passenger's side of the unmarked police car and walked over to it. He rested his hand on the engine.

"Cold."

"I'll take the back if you want the front."

"Sounds good."

On high alert, Mac crept up to the front door. Before Joe could get down the driveway, Mac called, "Joe. C'mere."

Joe walked up to his partner.

"Front door's open."

Mac eased open the door. Both men inched their way into the house. All was silent. Mac went into the front room while Joe proceeded down the hall. Overturned tables, books and papers strewn across the floor, couch cushions slashed and dislodged from their place greeted Mac's eyes. "Holy crap."

Joe called from the back of the house. "Mac. Back here."

Mac ran down the hall and into a back office. Crossing the threshold, he spotted Thomas Winslow seated at his desk, body spread across the blotter, blood spreading out from under his head and dripping onto the carpet. There was a hole in the back of his skull and his phone was in his hand. As Mac stepped closer to the desk, the cell rang. He took out a handkerchief from his pocket and removed it from Thomas's lifeless hand.

"Hello."

"Oh," said a female voice. "I'm looking for Thomas Winslow."

"I'm sorry, but Mr. Winslow is unable to come to the phone right now. Who's calling?"

"This is Audrey, his Executive Assistant. Mr. Winslow has an appointment with a client in a half hour. Does he wish me to cancel it?"

"Audrey, this is Detective MacKellar. We met earlier this morning."

"Yes, Detective. Is everything all right?"

"I'm afraid not. There's been an accident. Please inform the staff Mr. Winslow will not be in the office today. In fact, you should cancel his appointments for the next few days."

"Oh. I do hope he'll be okay."

"If you wouldn't mind staying at the office for a bit, we'll be back to talk to you as soon as we can."

Mac hung up the phone and put it on the desk.

"Shit. Better call it in."

While waiting for the forensic team, Mac surveyed the home office of the late Thomas Winslow. From his vantage point in the doorway, he let his sight pan the room. Small, but airy, there were French doors leading out to the garden behind the desk. Now, the doors stood wide open, the soft white sheers billowing in the breeze. A cozy reading alcove, with a table, bar and upholstered lounge chairs enclosed in a tent, was on the lush patio outside the door giving the room a much larger feel. Bookshelves and cabinets lined two of the walls. The desk sat mid room facing the door to the hall. Wanted to make sure he could see who entered the room. Mac slipped on his plastic gloves and walked closer to the desk, careful not to step in any blood. He examined the position of the arms, angle of the head and general demeanor of the body. He got down on his hands and knees on the rug and inspected the blood splatter that covered its surface. The door to the office opened. A pair of booties and the bottom edge of white coveralls came into view.

"Lose something, Detective?"

Mac jumped up and stared into Cissy's laughing eyes.

"Hi, Doc. Checking on the splatter pattern. Doesn't appear to be any defensive wounds on the hands. Don't think he saw it coming. I'd say he was seated at the desk, and someone came up behind and clobbered him. The house was ransacked but we don't know if anything is missing. I'm thinking the killer thought ol' Thomas had the will, and he wouldn't give it to them."

"Possibility."

"There's a nasty hole in the back of the skull and from the amount of blood, I'd say it happened a while ago."

"Well, I'll let you know once I've had him on my table."

"Thanks, I'd appreciate a call as soon as you know more detail. The killer's getting extremely nervous about that will and with the look of this, a bit desperate. By the mess out there, I don't think they found anything and that makes them even more treacherous. If a family member knows where the will is, they're in a lot of danger."

The forensic team gathered all the evidence and soon the body was on its way to the morgue.

"Ok, Mac. I'm off. I'll call you when I've got anything to report."

"Thanks, Doc. I'll talk to you in a bit."

Chapter Thirty-Nine

As Mac and Joe walked back to their car, a lady approached the pair.

"Excuse me. Is everything all right with Mr. Winslow?"

"And your name would be?"

"I'm Wanda Hargrave. I live across the street, and I noticed the police cars and all the activity at the Winslow's. Mrs. Winslow is away right now."

"Can you tell us anything about Mr. Winslow's activities this morning? Did he have any visitors?"

"Well, I saw his car was still in the driveway when I went out to do some shopping and it was still there when I came home. Struck me as odd 'cause he's usually gone by seven-thirty. There was another car in the driveway when I came home around ten, but after I put the groceries away and tidied up a bit, I looked out and it was gone."

"Do you know what kind of car it was?"

"Sorry, officer, but I don't know cars. It was silver if that helps."

"Did you happen to see the license plate?"

"Not really. It was one of those vanity plates though, but I don't remember what it said."

"Did you spot anything else?"

"No, although I think I saw a small red sports car parked in front of the house a little while later, but I can't say for sure. It could have been yesterday. Anyway, when I looked again it wasn't there. What's happened?"

"I'm afraid Mr. Winslow's had an accident."

"Oh, no. I hope he isn't hurt badly. I hope the couch and the rug are ok. Marjorie will be livid if they're damaged. They were delivered last week, and she's been showing them off to everyone. Had 'em specially made in time for a soiree she's holding next week. If they're ruined, they'll be hell to pay. Hrmph. Bit of a snob, if you ask me, but it's none

160

of my business."

"Thank you for your time, Ms. Hargrave. You've been very helpful. Here's my card. If you remember anything else, please give me a call."

"Detective MacKellar? No problem. Happy to help."

The men watched her walk back into her house.

"Always handy to have a nosy neighbor. Let's check out the silver sedan. See if anyone on our list has one. Also, the red sports car. It may be a long shot, but you never know."

By two o'clock, the men met in the office.

"Anything on the cars, Joe?"

"Yes. Fern Glen Developments own a couple of silver sedans, one of which is leased to Mr. Montgomery Carter, the CEO. The plates read "BILDRGHT"."

"Interesting. Let's take a ride."

Mac and Joe drove to the developer's headquarters in downtown Oshawa. Taking the elevator to the fifth floor, they stepped off into a luxurious foyer. A sign on the wall, behind the reception desk, announced you were in the rarified atmosphere of "Fern Glen Group, Inc., Ontario's number one builder of fine homes and condominiums". Pictures of current projects all over Ontario were displayed on the adjacent walls. Book racks featured pamphlets containing stellar reviews of the exquisite work and attention to detail on which Fern Glen Group prided themselves. The detectives approached the front desk.

"Detectives MacKellar and Surrey. We'd like to see Mr. Montgomery Carter."

"Do you have an appointment?"

"No."

"I'm sorry, Detective, but Mr. Carter is very busy and won't have time to see you this morning."

"This is not a courtesy call, Ms.?"

"Swanson."

"Swanson. I must insist that we speak to Mr. Carter now."

"I will buzz through, but he's with a client and doesn't want to be disturbed."

"You do that. We'll wait."

The receptionist buzzed through to the inner sanctum.

"Yes, I'm sorry, sir, but a Detective MacKellar and Detective Surrey insist they must see you right away."

She listened for a minute, then replied. "I don't know, sir. Detective MacKellar said he must speak with you, and I was to call you immediately. Yes, sir. I'll tell him."

She hung up the phone and spoke to Mac. "Detective, Mr. Carter will be right out."

After cooling their heels for about ten minutes, they watched a man walk through the inner door. He strode over to the detectives.

"Montgomery Carter," he said holding out his hand. "What's this all about, Detective. I'm a busy man and am in an important meeting now."

Mac shook his hand. "Do you have somewhere we could talk privately?"

"Follow me."

Carter turned on his heel and marched back through the door he had exited. The men followed him down a long hall and into a boardroom. Carter shut the door and turned to the men. "Alright, what's this all about?"

"Where were you this morning around ten o'clock?"

"What do you want to know that for?"

"Answer the question."

"I think I was at an appointment, although you could check with my Assistant."

"That appointment didn't happen to be with Thomas Winslow, did it?"

"Who?"

"Thomas Winslow. The lawyer for the Bancroft estate. The one you're trying to buy."

"Oh, him. I deal with many lawyers, it's hard to keep them all straight," Carter chuckled. "Names all begin to run together after a while."

"Oh, I think you'd remember him, since you lent or gave him one hundred thousand dollars to help you get hold of the property. Didn't quite work out the way you wanted, did it?"

"I beg your pardon. I don't know where you got your information, but I am not in the habit of paying to get hold of a property. I prefer to deal directly with the owner."

"Right and when she wouldn't sell, you thought a little intimidation might work. Yes, we know about the visit to the ranch last spring and a few misadventures which happened in the following months. That didn't work either, so you cozied up to Mr. Winslow. Perfect partner. You pay off his gambling debt, he gets the old lady to sell. Again, I ask, how did that work out for you?"

"Lovely fantasy, Detective, but I have no idea what you are talking about. Now, if you will excuse me, I have important work to do."

"Your car was seen at Winslow's house around ten o'clock this morning. We arrived at noon, to find the front and back door open, the house trashed, and Mr. Winslow's body was in his office with his head smashed in. Now, I ask you again, where were you at ten o'clock this morning?"

"His head smashed in?"

"Yes. He's quite dead."

Carter took a step backward and sat down. His mouth dropped open, and beads of sweat formed on his forehead. "Dead? He was fine when I left him."

"You were there?"

"Yes. My Associate, Harry Bales, and I went out to visit him this morning."

163

"What did you talk about?"

"Winslow and I have been working together for months to get the old lady to change her mind about selling. He introduced me to the son, Andrew. He and I agreed it was in the best interest of the family to sell me most of the estate. The family would receive a pretty penny for the sale, and I would be able to build a great community for the people of Durham. It was a win/win situation. Except for Mrs. Bancroft. She had a silly notion of preserving the land and opening a horse sanctuary for the nags on their way to the slaughterhouse. The three of us were working on changing her mind, but the plan didn't include murder. Thomas told me about the party and the discussion about a new will a while back, but he said he didn't know what happened to it. Mrs. Bancroft took it with her that night and no one has seen it since."

"You didn't decide to check his house to see if he was lying?"

"No. When Harry and I left he was very much alive. He didn't deliver on our deal. I wanted my hundred grand back, and I didn't care how he got it. He agreed but asked for a little more time to find the will. If found he'd destroy it. Then we could make the deal with Andrew Bancroft. That's how we left it. I didn't kill him."

"Okay, Mr. Carter. Thanks for your co-operation. If we have any further questions. We'll be in touch."

Chapter Forty

Mac closed his notebook and he and Joe walked out of the office. Climbing into their car, Joe clicked on his seat belt and asked, "Whadda ya think?"

"Gut feeling. He didn't do it. Too much at stake and whoever trashed the place was in a rage. That was not a methodical, reasoned search. Let's keep on checking the red sports car. I'll need to get the family together and tell them about Winslow. That should be fun."

Once more the family assembled in the living room of the house. Martha and Gladys took up their spots near the top of the curtains. Mac and Joe entered the room.

"What's this all about, Detective?" asked Andrew. "Has there been a break in Mother's case?"

"No, Mr. Bancroft. I called you all here this evening to inform you Mr. Thomas Winslow was murdered at his home today."

"What?" shouted everyone at once.

"This is all too much," said Adele, pulling out her handkerchief and waving it in front of her face. "I don't know how much more stress I can take. This whole ordeal will be the death of me."

"It's all right, Mommy. I'll take care of you," murmured Percy, patting his mother's arm.

The rest of the family sat in stunned silence. The two spirits felt a shock wave of fear spread throughout the room. Martha questioned Gladys. "Tom? Murdered? How come we haven't seen him?"

"We weren't with him when he died. A being from his own group or the Herdsmen will have met him."

"The Herdsmen?"

"They're the escorts for the darker realms. They stay with a soul even there, always encouraging them to turn to the light," Gladys said.

"Well, if he was the one who killed me, he deserves to go to the lower realms."

"It's not up to us to judge who goes where. We go where our energy resonates the best. If I'm resonating at a faster frequency, I can't function in a place of a lower density and vice versa. We belong in the light, but it's our choice whether to embrace it or not."

"I wonder why anyone would want to hurt him?"

"Dunno. Mac will tell us."

They turned their attention back to the assembly. Andrew was speaking.

"What has Winslow's murder got to do with my mother?"

"How was he killed?" asked Jared.

"Who would want to kill the lawyer, for heaven's sake?" inquired Adele.

Mac held up his hand to stop the barrage of questions. "That's a very good question, Mrs. Bancroft," said Mac turning to face her. "Who indeed?"

"Well, don't look at me," she replied.

"Really, Detective," sniffed Percy. "My mother is completely incapable of violence. She has a sensitive constitution, and any kind of ugliness upsets her terribly."

"Arrrgghh. Shut up. You're so annoying," screamed Martha. The picture above the mantle started to shake. Mac looked at it. *Hmm. Maybe Martha's hanging around after all.*

"I wasn't suspecting you Mrs. Bancroft. My apologies if you thought I was."

"Well, I should think not. A respectable woman such as I," she exhaled.

"Getting back to Dr. Bancroft's question, Mr. Winslow was found seated at a desk in his office at home with his head bashed in."

"Oh, how terrible," cried Vanessa. "I don't like this, Andy. I'm frightened."

Andrew picked up his wife's hands and began to rub them. "It's ok, sweetheart. I won't let anything happen to you."

Mac looked over the group taking in all their expressions and body language. "Did any of you see Mr. Winslow in the last few days?"

"No," said the group.

"Do you have any idea why he may have been killed?"

"No," they said in unison.

"Odd timing, doncha think?"

"How so," asked Jared?

"Mrs. Bancroft was killed a month ago on the eve of discussing a new will. The will vanished and no one has seen it since. Mr. Winslow was Mrs. Bancroft's attorney and had the will in his possession at some point. Perhaps the murderer assumed he had it all along and went looking for it. Mr. Winslow's house was ransacked. Either the killer was searching for it and Mr. Winslow interrupted him or the killer went on a rampage after questioning him and not receiving the answer he wanted. Either way, we still don't know where it is. I'll need access to the house again, Mr. Bancroft."

"That's outrageous. Winslow's murder may have nothing at all to do with my mother's death. How long are we going to be subjected to these so-called searches, Detective? They're extremely upsetting to everyone."

"Until we find the will. This is the last place it was seen. We start here. There's a good chance the two cases are connected. We'll be investigating with that premise in mind."

Martha's energy began to spike as she listened to Mac. "Gladys, we have to get Mac's attention to help him find the will."

"Calm down. You're shooting sparks. So how to you propose we do that?"

"He said he's coming back to search again. I've got to make him understand I'm here and want to help. This being in spirit is a pain sometimes. I miss my body and being able to touch things and talk to people."

"You've been practicing manipulating the energy. What about materializing?"

"I'm almost there. Sure uses a lot of power. Let's go back to my room and practice. I'll do it if it kills me. Oh right. I'm already dead."

Chapter Forty-One

A torrential downpour let loose as Mac fired up the car and drove to Thor's Sanctuary. Parking at the top of the curved driveway, he opened the door and made a mad dash for the entrance to the house. The door opened and Rebecca rushed him inside.

"Nice to see you again Mac. C'mon back into the kitchen. We're just warming up with a cuppa."

"Thanks. I could use a good cup. The stuff at the office is pure sludge."

Rebecca and Mac walked into the kitchen where Cissy was sitting at the kitchen table sipping her coffee.

"Hey Mac," she called. "Great day for a ghost hunt."

At that precise moment, a crack of lightening and boom of thunder shook the house rattling the dishes and windows. Everyone jumped.

Cissy placed her hand on her heart. "My God. Martha knows we're coming."

"Not funny, Cissy," replied Becca. "Are you guys sure you want to go today?"

"C'mon, Becca. Don't be silly. You've seen ghosts before. Who knows? Maybe it was a one-time deal, and you won't see or feel Martha."

"Yeah, well, once in a lifetime was enough for me."

"We don't have to do this, ladies," stated Mac.

"No, that's ok. I must admit, I am curious, but I do wish it were sunny."

"Let's grab our Java and be on our way."

The threesome picked up their travel mugs and walked to the door. The rain had lessened to a slow drizzle. Pulling up the collar of his coat, Mac opened the door. "Ladies," he said, stepping back and escorting them to the car. Once everyone was settled, he drove them to the estate.

"Wow," said Rebecca. "I've seen this from the roadway hundreds of times, but it's even more impressive up close."

"Ready to go in?" asked Cissy.

"Let's do this."

The trio exited the car and walked up to the front porch. Mac rang the bell. After a few minutes, they could hear footsteps walking across the tile foyer. The door opened and Charli was there.

"Detective MacKellar. Dad said you'd be coming today."

"Thank you, Ms. Bancroft. This is Dr. Walsh, the Coroner and Mrs. Connacher. We won't be long."

Charli shuddered. "Are you making any progress on finding out who killed my grandmother?"

"All in due course, Ms. Bancroft."

"That's an answer that's not an answer if I ever heard one. Come in. I'll be out the back at the stables if you need anything." Charli turned from the group and strode down the hall and through the kitchen doors.

"Not impressed with our work, I see," said Cissy.

"Doesn't like the fact her brother's still under suspicion. Getting back to why we're here… sensing anything, Rebecca?"

"No. Nothing. Let's go further into the house and see what I feel."

Mac led the way to the living room. "This is where the family was gathered the night I told them about her death."

Rebecca stood still in the doorway and concentrated her mind. She couldn't feel a thing. "This is ridiculous," she muttered to herself. "I haven't a clue what I'm supposed to feel or look for." Clasping her hands behind her back, she began to wander about the room. Out of the corner of her eye, she picked up movement. She turned her head and looked at the curtains. Up in the top corner of the drapes, back in the shadows, she saw a tiny pinpoint of light. As she gazed at it, it began to move up and down. Fascinated, she watched as it slowly moved out from the curtains and came to rest near a small desk under the window. A pen, laying on the desk began to shake, and it rolled off the table onto

170

the carpet. The room filled with a mist, like it had at Stone Cottage. An elegant elderly lady, wearing a blue dress and leaning on a cane materialized in front of her. She pointed to Rebecca, pointed upstairs, and vanished along with the mist. Cissy and Mac rushed over to her. "Becca, are you alright?"

"Did you see her?" Becca asked.

"Who?"

"The woman in the blue dress."

"No. I could tell you were seeing something as you started to sway, and your face turned white. Did you see anything, Mac?"

"No. Tell me exactly what you saw Rebecca."

Rebecca described what she had seen. "I presume it was Martha?"

"Sounds like the dress she wore when they buried her. What did she do?"

"She pointed at me, pointed upstairs and then disappeared. She wants us to go to her room."

"Ok. Let's move."

The small band went up the stairs, along the hall and entered Martha's room. A stale, musty smell assaulted their noses. Mac walked across the rug, opened the curtains and the windows, and then turned back to the women. "Well, now what?"

"I don't know. I've never done this before. I told you I only had one experience. I don't know if I can do anything again."

"Give her a break, Mac. None of us have much knowledge when it comes to stuff like this. Let's wait and see what happens."

Mac grunted and sat at Martha's desk. "Where would she have put it?"

"You looked all through this room and the walk-in closet," asked Becca?

"Do I look stupid?"

"Don't get testy. Just making sure we're on the same page. How about under the desk? Taped to the bottom?"

"You've been watching too many movies."

"Humor me."

"This desk was turned inside out as well as the tables by the bed and the bookcase. Nothing."

"Ok. Is there a safe in the room?"

As Becca asked the question, the lamp on the bedside table wobbled and fell onto the floor. "Well, I'll take that as a 'yes'."

"We searched everywhere but couldn't find it."

A pen on the desk wobbled and rolled into Mac's lap. He jumped, knocking over the chair, and causing the pen to fall on his foot. "Jesus," he shouted. "Let's get this over with."

Cissy and Becca looked at each other and smiled. Trying to hide her laughter, Becca turned her head and spotted the bobbing light by the mantle of the fireplace. "Guys, Martha is here. Martha if that's you, can you bob up and down?" The light bounced twice. "Is there a safe in this room?" The light bounced again. "Where is it?" The light zoomed over to the mouth of the fireplace and bounced up and down.

"It must around that grate."

Mac strode over to the hearth and pulled the grate onto the floor. He stared at the tiles. "This ash has been moved. Hand me that shovel, will you?"

Cissy handed him the shovel and he scooped up the ash and put it in a bucket beside the fire irons. "I wonder if this tile moves." Placing the shovel under the edge of the tile, Mac pushed down on the handle and the tile moved up. "Well, well, what do we have here?" Lifting the tile away, Mac peered into the cavity. "Success, ladies. We have discovered Martha's safe. Now to open it."

"Maybe Martha can help." Addressing the ball of light, Becca asked, "Martha, can you bounce up and down to give us the combination?"

The ball bounced once.

"Okay. What's the first number?"

The ball bounced three times. "The first number is three?"

The ball bounced once. "Right. Now we have it. What's the second number?"

The ball bounced again. This went on until all six numbers to the lock were revealed. Mac tried the numbers and the box clicked open.

"Well, well. Lookey here."

Mac reached in and pulled out a manila envelope, opened it and shook out the contents. Unfolding one of the documents, he saw he held the Last Will and Testament of Martha Bancroft.

"Yes," shouted Martha doing a fist bump. "Da-da-da-da-dah-da feelin' groovy," she sang as she danced around the room. Increasing her energy, Martha apparated in front of the trio. She clapped her hands, sending them a big smile, then blew them all a kiss and vanished.

Mac dropped the will and fell back on his butt against the fireplace, his mouth dropping open. Cissy and Becca looked at each other and smiled. Cissy winked at her.

"Well, I guess the question about Martha hanging around has been answered."

Mac closed his mouth his eyes still glazed. "What just happened?"

"You, my dear sir, have had your first encounter with a ghost," replied Cissy with a chuckle. "Kinda neat, eh?"

"Holy shit," whispered Mac. He stayed where he was, trying to take a deep breath and swallowing furiously. Finally, he drew a lung full of air and his breathing returned to normal. Once he regained his equilibrium, he picked up the will and scanned it. His face broke into a grin. He closed his eyes and leaned back against the stone.

"It's signed and been witnessed by Mrs. Vanessa Bancroft. That's what she was hiding from me. Guess we'll have to have a little chat with our lovely Vanessa."

Chapter Forty-Two

The weather had cleared up by the time Mac dropped the women back at Thor's Sanctuary. "Thanks for your help, ladies. I appreciate it. Don't know how I'm going to explain finding the will, but I'll think of something. That was quite an experience. Guess there's more to life than what we can see with our eyes, but I think I'll leave all the ghostbuster stuff to others. Not really my cup of tea."

"Hear ya," replied Becca. "Glad I could be of service. Although I've now had two experiences of the other side, I'm with you in concentrating on the here and now."

"What a bunch of wimps! That was fun. Don't you want to know more about the great beyond?" Cissy teased.

"No," said Mac and Becca in unison.

"Ha ha," laughed Cissy. "Okay. Different strokes. Why don't we get lunch and talk about what we do now?"

"Sorry, Cissy, I have to get back to the office, but I'll take a rain check."

"No problem, Mac. Talk to you soon."

Becca and Cissy walked up to the house as Mac watched them go. *Man, that Doc sure turns my crank. Even with the spooks.* As Cissy turned to wave at Mac, he saluted her and climbed into his car. Driving back to the office, his mind played over the events of the morning. How was he going to explain finding the will? He could barely believe what happened and he was there. Shit. He'd have to think of a great story to tell Joe and the Captain. At least they had it. One mystery solved. It was signed and Vanessa had witnessed it. Must have happened when she took up the hot toddy to the old lady. I knew she wasn't telling all she knew. Must have been what she was trying to tell him at the family gathering. We'll have her in for a little chat to see if she knows anything else.

174

Mac arrived back at the station and signaled Joe to meet him in his office.

"What's up?"

"Went out to the Bancroft estate this morning for one last look around and look what I found." He pulled the evidence bag containing the will out of his jacket pocket.

"Holy crap. You found it. Where? Is it signed?"

"Yeah, it's signed and what's more it's been witnessed by Vanessa Bancroft."

"Vanessa?"

"Yup."

"That's what she's been hiding."

"Think we'd better bring her in for a little chat," said Mac as he picked up his phone and called Vanessa.

"Mrs. Bancroft, Detective MacKellar. I have a few more questions for you regarding your mother-in-law's death. I would appreciate it if you could come down to the station or if it's more convenient Detective Surrey and I can come to the ranch. Yes, we can be there in about a half an hour. We'll see you soon."

Vanessa hung up the phone and turned to leave the living room.

"Who was that," inquired Andrew strolling into the room.

"Detective MacKellar. He and his partner are coming out to the house 'cause he has a few more questions for me."

"Why would he want to question you? You don't know anything."

"You stupid man. You've no idea what I know or don't know. You're all puffed up with your own importance and trying to undo all

175

the good Mother wanted to do – you can't see what's right in front of you."

Andrew reached out to grab her arm, but she pushed him away. "Don't touch me. I'm going up to our room to take an aspirin. I have a blinding headache." Putting her hand to her mouth to stifle a sob, she ran out of the room and up the stairs. Andrew followed her calling, "Nessa. What did I do? Please come back and we can talk." The only sound he heard was the slamming of their bedroom door.

He walked to the library and the credenza. Pouring himself a liberal drink, he sank into one of the tub chairs by the fireplace. Cupping the glass in his hands, he tapped the side with his fingers while staring at the flames. The door opened and Percy stepped into the room.

"Uncle Andrew. I didn't realize you were home. Is everything ok? I thought I heard raised voices."

"That idiot detective is coming out to the house again to harass us with more questions. Honestly, we've told him everything we know, but he wants to grill Vanessa again."

"Vanessa?"

"Yeah. Can you believe it? I love her dearly, but she's not the brightest bulb in the box. As if she'd know anything. Ah well, he'll be along in a minute. I'd better get ready. I wish this whole mess were over. All I want is what's rightfully mine and to have the family comfortable, so we don't have to worry about money. Is that so wrong?"

"Not at all. I agree with you. Wonder where the will went. Do you have any idea what happened to it?"

"Nope. Haven't seen it since the meeting. Maybe she ripped it up. God, I hope so. It would make things much simpler."

"I hear you. Well, I'm off to see the Maestro. Hopefully, we'll still be able to salvage our trip this summer. Ta da."

Percy left the room. Andrew heard the front door shut a few minutes later. Lost in his thoughts, he sat in the quiet warmth of the room. He had no idea how long he had been there when he heard the front doorbell chime. Rising from his chair he went to answer the door.

"Detectives. My wife said that you would be coming. What do you want now?"

"We have new evidence in the case, Mr. Bancroft and need to ask your wife a few questions. Would you get her please?"

Andrew's shoulders slumped in resignation. "I'm sure you know the way to the library. I'll get my wife." The two men followed him into the house. As he went to collect Vanessa, they continued down the hall. After a few minutes, the door opened. Andrew, holding his wife's hand, led her into the room and sat her in a comfortable chair in front of the fire.

"Gentlemen. I insist on staying in the room for the interview. My wife suffers from migraines and is fragile right now."

"We have no problem with you being here, Mr. Bancroft, as long as it's okay with Mrs. Bancroft."

Vanessa nodded her head, leaned back in the chair, and closed her eyes.

"The last few times we've been together, Mrs. Bancroft, you seemed as if you might have had something on your mind. Is there anything you wish to tell us?"

"No, detective. I've told you everything I know."

"Really?" Mac pulled out the will from his inner jacket pocket and laid it on the table between them.

Vanessa's eyes opened wide, and her mouth formed a small 'o'. "You found it!"

"Yes, ma'am. Now do you have anything to say?"

Andrew grabbed up the paper. "What is this?" He looked it over, his face turning red and his brow furrowing into a scowl. "Is this the new will?" He flipped over to the final page. "It's been signed and witnessed. Vanessa, why didn't you tell me you had witnessed Mother's signature?"

"I couldn't. I promised Mother I wouldn't tell anyone about what I'd done. She especially didn't want me to tell you. She said she'd explain in the morning, but then by morning she was dead, and I didn't know what to do." Vanessa burst into tears.

"Mrs. Bancroft, did you know where the will has been all this time?"

"No. After I signed it, I kissed Mother goodnight. When I was about to leave, I turned around to look at her. She was leaning back in the bed. She had closed her eyes and was holding the paper against her chest. I knew it had been a hard decision for her. I didn't want to disturb her, so I left."

"Are you now quite sure you've told us everything you know about this case?"

"There is another thing, but I can't quite remember. About when I was in the kitchen getting the hot toddy. It's there at the corner of my memory, but I can't quite get it. I'm sorry, detective, that's all I know."

"Thank you, Mrs. Bancroft. That will be all for now. We'll show ourselves out." The detectives got up from their positions and exited to room.

The crackling of the fire was the only sound heard in the library. Andrew walked to the chair where Vanessa was sitting and squatted down in front of her. Taking her cold hands in his, he began to rub them to bring warmth back into her body.

"Nessa. Why didn't you tell me about the will?"

"I told you. I promised Mother I wouldn't."

"But after she died, surely that promise didn't matter anymore."

"Why should I tell you? All you wanted to do was destroy it. You didn't want Mother's wishes to go through. After all these years, I finally see through you, Andrew Bancroft. You're just interested in being a big shot. Well, I've had enough. I found out I can only do so much shopping before I get bored. Who knew? I liked Mother's ideas. She was going to find a place for me to work and help. I didn't want you to make a mess of it all."

Vanessa bent over, her face in her hands. Sobs, as if her very soul was being torn apart, escaped from her lips, as her body shook from the

178

ferocity of her anguish. Andrew rose on his knees and gathered his wife into his arms.

"Oh, Nessa. I'm sorry. I wanted to make you proud of me and to give you all the beautiful things that you've never had."

"No," she said her voice muffled against Andrew's chest. "You wanted me to look good for all your cronies. I've heard them talk. A 'trophy wife' is what I'm called. A bimbo, gold digger… you name it. I've heard them all and I'm tired of it. I want to prove to everyone I'm just as good as everyone else. Mother was going to give me a chance, but you would've taken it away." She wriggled herself out of Andrew's arms and stood, hands on hips, facing him. "I need to think. I'm going for a walk."

Andrew grabbed her arm. "Nessa. Wait."

Vanessa pushed Andrew back breaking his grip. "Don't you ever grab me like that again! I said I'm going for a walk. Don't try to follow me or come with me. I need to be alone. We'll talk when I get back."

Andrew stood, shoulders drooped, listening to his wife call for Zeus. He could hear her murmuring soothing phrases to him and the click of his leash as it was attached to his harness. Then he heard the squeak of the closet door where she hung her coat. Heels clicked across the foyer and the final sound he heard was the front door slamming shut.

Chapter Forty-Three

Vanessa walked away from the ranch and down Ashburn Road. What was she going to do? She loved Andy, but he'd grown arrogant and stuffy the last few years. She wanted the fun-loving man she married back. Could it happen? Lost in thought, Vanessa was not aware of the car coming up behind her. She felt it hit her and then she was flying only to land skidding to a stop on the rough pavement. All went black.

Andrew remained in the library, unaware of the tears spilling from his eyes and landing in his lap. The sound of a dog barking broke through his reverie.

That's Zeus. Why is he barking? He went with Vanessa. What's he doing back at the house?

Andrew jumped from his chair, wiped his eyes, and hurried to the front door. Pulling it open, he saw the little dog, his leash trailing behind, running in circles on the porch and barking. When he saw Andrew, he ran down the steps, turned and barked and ran father down the driveway. "What's the matter, Zeus? Where's Vanessa?"

Zeus ran back to him, barked, turned and again, ran down the driveway.

Figuring the animal wanted him to follow, Andrew grabbed his coat and ran after the dog. "Where's Vanessa, Zeus? Find Vanessa."

Dog and man ran down the road until Andrew spotted a heap of what looked like Vanessa's coat lying at the edge of the road. He ran up to it. "Oh, my God. No. Vanessa. Can you hear me sweetheart?" He wiped the blood-stained hair from her face and felt for a pulse. It was faint, but it was there. Reaching into his pocket, he pulled out his cell and called 911. Then he called Mac.

"Detective MacKellar. This is Andrew Bancroft. My wife has been in an accident. No, she's still breathing, but she won't wake up. I'm on Ashburn Road below the ranch. I've called the ambulance. They should be here in minutes. They'll take her to Lakeridge Health in Oshawa. I'll meet you there."

The ambulance soon arrived and whisked Vanessa to the hospital, where she was rushed into emergency. Andrew arrived a short time later, along with Mac and Joe.

"What happened," asked Mac rushing up to Andrew at the emergency desk?

"I don't know. Nessa decided to go for a walk with Zeus. A little while later, Zeus came back on his own, barking and carrying on. I followed him and he led me to Vanessa who was lying on the side of the road." He slumped down into one of the chairs in the waiting area and hunched over with his head in his hands. After about an hour, the doors to the emergency department swung open and a doctor came through.

"Mr. Bancroft?"

"Yes. I'm Andrew Bancroft."

"Dr. Grainger. Your wife has sustained a concussion. There are several contusions and there may be internal damage. We will be doing tests to determine the extent of her injuries, but I am most concerned about the trauma to her head. After the tests, we will move her to the ICU where she can be monitored closely until she regains consciousness."

"She will be alright, though, right?"

"We'll do our best."

"Can I see her?"

"Certainly, Mr. Bancroft. You can stay in the room with her."

"Thank you."

Dr. Grainger turned and walked back into the department. Andrew followed. Mac watched them go.

181

"Stay here and get what info you can from the paramedics and doctor. I'm going to the accident scene to see what I can find out. I don't like this, Joe. No sooner had we finished interviewing her than she has an accident?"

"Not sure it was an accident?"

"No. Little too convenient, I'd say. I'm going to call the office. Get a guard put on her room. I don't want to take any chances."

Chapter Forty-Four

She could hear people talking but couldn't open her eyes or move any part of her body. What were they saying?

"Vanessa, dear, you can come out now."

Come out? Come out where?

An intense white light surrounded her, and she felt herself lifting from a prone to a standing position. The light dimmed and she saw Martha and another person standing with her.

"Mother Bancroft?"

"Yes, dear. This is Gladys. A friend of mine."

"Am I dead?"

"No, you're in a coma."

"What happened to me?"

"A car hit you on your walk."

"Is Zeus okay?" she asked.

"Yes, he's fine. He ran back to the house to get Drew. He saved you."

"Really? What a good boy. Everything's a bit fuzzy, but I remember the police were at the house. They found the will. Andy was terribly angry with me for not telling him about it."

"I know. I was the one who led them to it. I'm sorry about Drew. I should never have made you promise a thing like that."

"Oh, but you were right. If he had known, he would have destroyed it, and all your beautiful dreams would be gone."

"I wonder if that would be so bad."

"Yes, it would be horrible. I argued with Andy about it. I told him I wanted the ranch to be as you wanted it."

"Yes, we heard."

"Oh, you were there?"

"Yes. Gladys and I have been here this whole time."

"Why?"

"I want to find out who killed me and why."

"Oh, I don't know that… although there is something about making your toddy that's eating at me. I should remember but can't. I'll think of it when I wake up. I will wake up, won't I?"

"Yes, dear. It's not your time.

"I'm glad to see you again."

"I'm glad to see you too, Vanessa. I wanted to apologize for the way I've treated you all these years. You're a gentle, kind soul and I was wrong. I've grown to love and appreciate you since I died. You're good for my son and I'm glad he has you. Let him know I love him and wish we had more time together. Help him see the things that are important in life."

"Thank you, Mother. All I've ever wanted is your love and respect. I'll take good care of both Andy and Zeus."

"Would you call me something else instead of 'Mother'? It sounds so stuffy."

Vanessa's essence brightened so it looked like she was standing in a spotlight. Her face was beaming with a huge smile. "I'd love that too. I sure wish we had more time together to go shopping or… or something… Mom. Gosh, it feels good to call you Mom."

Martha's figure glowed stronger and she smiled at her daughter-in-law. "I'm glad we got that settled. I feel much better. Would you also let Jared know I approve of his relationship with Kelly?"

"Who's Kelly?"

"A friend. He's been with her for at least a year, but he was worried I wouldn't like her because she comes from a lower class like... er."

"Like me?" Vanessa whispered.

Martha's light dimmed a little. "I was thinking more of Adele, but you too. I'm learning, though."

"It's okay, Mom. I know you love me, and all that other stuff is in the past. I'll be happy to let him know you approve, but how can I tell

184

him? I can't very well say that I've been talking to your ghost."

"Tell him I knew about the situation, and we talked about it when you signed the will. I wanted to approach him but didn't know how. You'll figure it out. I believe in you. Gladys and I will be staying around for a bit to see how the investigation goes, then I'll be moving on to find Bobby and Ed. I'll be watching over you when we get home. Take care of yourself and watch for signs I'm with you."

"I will. I love you, Mom. Have a nice trip."

Martha and Gladys faded away and Vanessa felt herself sucked back into the body on the bed. Her hand started to twitch. Andrew lying with his head on her hand, felt it move. Lifting his head, he called to her.

"Nessa. Sweetheart, can you hear me? Come back, baby. C'mon. Open those beautiful eyes."

Vanessa stirred and let out a deep sigh.

Andrew ran to the door. "Help. Help! My wife's waking up."

Nurses and attendants hurried toward Vanessa's room and pulled the curtain around her.

"I'm sorry, Mr. Bancroft, but you will need to wait in the hall."

"No, I need to be with her."

"I'm sorry, sir. Let us do our job and you'll be with her as quickly as we can find out what's happening."

Andrew left the room to pace in front of her door. As he was waiting, a uniformed officer placed a chair beside the door and took a seat. Startled, Andrew asked, "Why are you here?"

"Detective MacKellar requested a watch detail for Mrs. Bancroft."

"It was an accident, wasn't it?"

"That's what he's trying to find out. Don't want to take any chances."

"Oh, my God. This is a nightmare. My mother, Winslow and now my wife? Who would do this? What's happening?"

He paced again, pushing his hand through his hair, shaking with agitation. After what seemed like an eternity, the door opened, and a doctor came toward him.

"Everything is fine, Mr. Bancroft. Your wife has regained consciousness and is resting comfortably. You can see her now, but don't stay too long as she is tired and needs her rest. We'll move her to a regular room tomorrow and if all goes well, she'll be home later in the week."

"Thank you, doctor. I'll take it easy."

Andrew entered Vanessa's room, walked up to the bed, and sat in the chair next to it. He took Vanessa's hand in his own and smiled.

"Hi, Sweetheart. You scared the beejesus out of me. I thought I'd lost you."

"Would it have mattered?"

"Mattered? You're my whole life. I don't know what I'd do without you."

"Really?"

Andrew hung his head. "I know it hasn't seemed like it this past while, but I do love you. Please forgive me." He looked at his wife, tears pooling in his eyelids. "I've never felt loved before you. Please don't leave me. I couldn't bear it."

"Andy, I love you too and so did your mother."

"Hah."

"She did. She told me. She was also deeply sorry about the way she treated both of us and wanted to make amends."

"When did she tell you this? When you took her the toddy?"

"Around then, but she did tell me, and you need to know it. I'd like to put our marriage back together, Andy, but there must be changes made in the way we live. I love that old house. I don't want the land changed into a bunch of houses all looking the same. All that noise and traffic. It would spoil everything. Please don't fight the will."

"We'll talk about it when you are stronger, but I'm inclined to agree with you. All the death and ugliness. Over a piece of land. You could have died today. It's not worth it."

"Thank you, Andy Panda." Vanessa lifted her hand to stroke

186

Andrew's cheek, her eyes shining with happy tears.

"The doctor says you will be moved tomorrow and if all goes well, you can come home later this week. Won't that be great?"

Vanessa crinkled her nose and sniffed the air. "With the antiseptic smell in here, I will be very glad to be at the house in our own bed with fresh air coming in the window."

Andrew moved to the bed and gently lifted his wife into his arms. He placed her head on his chest and kissed her brow. Brushing her hair back from her cheek, he looked with deep desire into his wife's trusting eyes and smiled. "And there's no place I would rather have you," he said before laying a gentle kiss on her soft lips.

Chapter Forty-Five

The weather was unusually warm for late November when Cissy joined Mac on his deck for a morning coffee.

"Good morning, Doc. You look lovely as usual," he smiled at her.

"Thank you, kind sir... and thanks for the invite to join you this morning."

"I wanted to go over the case with you. Let you know what's happening. Vanessa Bancroft left the hospital day before yesterday. She had a dislocated shoulder, a few bruised ribs, minor internal injuries and cuts and scrapes, but otherwise, she'll be fine. She was fortunate the car didn't hit her head on. She was walking south on Ashburn and was hit from behind. There were no skid marks on the road. The car didn't even try to stop. It had to cross the road to strike her. This is a deliberate case of attempted murder. But the reconstruction team said there was a large pothole at the curb ahead of the spot where she was hit. They figure the driver hit the pothole, lost control, and only glanced her right side. If it had been a full impact, she'd be dead."

"Why would anyone want to kill her? The will has been found. Trying to stop Mrs. Bancroft's plans is pointless."

"The last time I talked to her, she was trying to remember exactly what happened on the night of her mother-in-law's murder. It was tickling the back of her mind, but she couldn't quite bring it to the front. Maybe the killer suspects what she knows will incriminate them and wants to stop her."

"Here's the autopsy report on Thomas Winslow. Cause of death was blunt force trauma to the skull. Forensics found a statue in the garden. The killer tried to make it look like it belonged, but a sharp-eyed technician noticed the soil had around it had been disturbed. When she lifted it up, they discovered traces of hair and blood. They matched

Winslow's, so we found our murder weapon. We also found a spot on the bookcase near the desk where something was removed. The shape in the dust is the same shape as the statue. No sign of forced entry. Probably a person who knew Winslow or he would've raised the alarm. Nothing appears to have been taken. His laptop, cell and other electronics are still in the house. Doesn't appear to be a burglary gone bad."

"My gut says it's to do with the will. Somebody thought Winslow was lying when he said he didn't have it and he was killed for it, but who? Think I'll go out to the estate. I'd like to make sure Mrs. Bancroft's okay and see if she can remember what it is she wanted to tell me. Want to tag along?"

"Sure, I'm game."

Mac smiled. "Yeah, you sure are. Remember as soon as this case is over, Ms. Walsh, I intend to whisk you away on a romantic evening for two at one of Toronto's finest restaurants. Perhaps the 360 at the CN Tower?"

"You're on, Mr. MacKellar. I'm looking forward to it."

As the two made their way to Mac's car, his cell rang.

"Joe."

"Mac. Got something. The forensics boys found a fresh paint scrape on a tree near the scene of Mrs. Bancroft's hit and run. They bagged it and ran tests. It belongs to a late model car."

"Color?"

"Red."

"Same as the elusive car from Winslow's place."

"Yup and it matches a 2015 Corvette. Guess who owns a 2015 Corvette. Percy Bancroft."

"Percy?"

"Yup."

"The Doc and I are on our way to the house to see Mrs. Bancroft. Get a warrant and meet us there. We'll check the garage and then have a little chat with Percy."

"Sure thing."

Hanging up, Mac turned to Cissy. "The car that hit Vanessa also scraped a tree. Forensics found it's a 2015 red Corvette. Joe discovered Percy owns such a car, so we'll question him while we are at the ranch."

Chapter Forty-Six

Mac drove through the gates of the estate and down a lane to the garages. He and Cissy exited the car. She walked over to the fence and rested her arms on the top rail. Mac joined her.

"Penny?"

"I was thinking about this place. It's so beautiful. Martha had some great plans. From all I've heard, Jared is an excellent vet and will make a great custodian for the property. Those unwanted horses will have a wonderful home. It would be a shame if Andrew fights the new will and gets his way."

"There's nothing we can do about it."

"I know, but I'd love to be able to drive by here and still see these fields and animals instead of a bunch of houses."

"I hear ya."

The sound of an approaching car interrupted their conversation. Mac turned from the fence and walked over to where Joe was pulling in.

"I got the warrant."

"Good job," replied Mac.

Cissy wandered over to join the detectives and the trio made their way into the garage. Flicking on a light, they saw that of the six bays in the building, only one slot was empty.

"Shit. We missed him," said Joe, striding to the empty stall.

"I don't think so," said Mac, walking past Joe to the bay at the far end of the garage. "I think it's down here. I can see a tiny flash of red in that end bay. You can't see it from where you're standing. See. There. Behind the F-150."

Joe moved to the end of the bay. "I see it now. You're right. Let's see what we've got." He joined Mac and they made their way to the end bay where a sleek red corvette was parked. Joe whistled. "Beauty," he said caressing the car.

"Over here," said Mac who was crouched by the passenger's side bumper. Joe walked over and bent down to see where Mac was pointing.

"Aha," he said. "A little front-end damage on her. Whoever did this should be shot!"

"Take a sample, Joe and then we'd better have a talk with Percy. Looks like he's got some splainin' to do. Come to the house as soon as you're finished here."

Joe pulled an evidence bag out of his pocket and with his pocketknife peeled a couple of paint chips from the damaged car. Mac went back to Cissy and the two of them left the building.

"Let's go to the house before Percy figures out we're on to him and makes a run for it."

"After you, Captain," said Cissy.

The pair started to walk up the path towards the house when they heard a faint scream. They stopped in their tracks.

"What was that," asked Cissy?

"Don't know but it sounded like a scream. Let's move it. Joe, c'mon. Something's going on at the house."

Chapter Forty-Seven

L ost deep in thought, Vanessa paced the floor of her bedroom. At first, she didn't hear the click of the door or the stealthy approach. The squeak of a floorboard penetrated her mind, and she looked up.

"Adele. This is a surprise. I was going to look for you."

"Really, my dear. How can I help?"

"It's about the night of Mother's party. There's something I've been trying to remember. It's probably important, but I just can't think of what it is."

Adele moved closer to Vanessa. "Let's see if we can figure it out together, shall we?"

Vanessa's eyes widened and she gasped as Adele drew near. "Your perfume. That's it! When I made Mother's toddy, I remembered hearing a noise in the pantry and I left the drink on the table while I went to check it out. When I came back to the kitchen, I could smell your fragrance although I didn't realize it at the time. That's what I've been trying to remember. You were there. You were in the kitchen. Why didn't you say anything?"

"I suspected you saw or heard something that night, but being the silly bimbo you are, I wasn't surprised you couldn't remember what it was. I was listening at the door when you talked to that detective. I knew I only had a little time to stop you before you remembered. You've made it difficult for me."

"What do you mean?"

"I got Percy's car and followed you when you went for your walk. Percy took my Caddy as he wanted the bigger car to impress his friends."

"That, was you?"

"Yes, and it would've worked too if it wasn't for that pothole. I didn't see it until it was too late, and I landed in it. Jerked the wheel right out of my hands and I only bumped your side. The car glanced off a tree on the other side of the road before I could get control of it again. Stupid roads. They really need to fix them more often. I shall have to complain to the works department. That's what we pay taxes for. Percy will be furious when he sees the damage. So far, I've managed to hide it from him. But I digress. Where were we? Oh yes, the night of Martha's party."

"I wanted to know why you didn't say anything to me in the kitchen. It doesn't make any sense, unless…"

"Yes?"

"You didn't want me to know you were there. You were the one who poisoned the toddy."

"Clever little girl, aren't you? It was simple. I know all about the drug from Percy. He and his young friends have experimented with several different things to enhance their musical ability. He explained how it started out as an animal tranquilizer, but in humans in can cause wonderful feelings of ecstasy, joining with the universe and all that other crap. He told me you must be careful because an overdose can be quite lethal. After Martha told us about her new plans, I knew I had to stop her. Since Jared's a vet, I thought he might have some, so I went to his office. The keys to the cupboard were in the desk drawer, so I opened it and there was a bottle of the lovely poison. Perfect solution. One bottle had even been opened. I took it out and poured a little in a vial I found in the drawer with the keys. It only took a minute, and no one saw me. I was going to use it the next day, but as I was coming back to the house, I saw you making the toddy through the window. Perfect opportunity. When you left the kitchen, I slipped in, emptied the vial into the mug and left again. Then I went to the library to get a well-deserved drink. It only took a few minutes, and no one was the wiser."

"But why? What did she ever do to you?"

"I've hated her for years. Always demanding we jump at her

command. Always loving her golden boy better than mine. My son is every bit as good as Jared is, but she could never see it. In fact, Percy's better. He's going to be a great musician and she had no right to take away that opportunity from him. He'll be known all over the world in the best circles, but she called the Maestro a fraud. How dare she! My son is worth ten times what Jared is. Matriarch of the clan! Ha. I'll make a much better mistress of this house than she ever was. I expected her death to be put down to old age, but the coroner decided to do an autopsy. Hadn't counted on that."

"Did you tamper with her truck?"

"I was furious when the detective said she was going to do an autopsy. I knew she'd find the poison. I saw her sitting in the kitchen after my interview, so I snuck out of the house and cut the brake line. My dad was a mechanic, and I learned a lot about cars and trucks as a kid. I used to help him on the weekends. Easy-peasy. It was a mistake, but she made me so angry I wasn't thinking straight. Oh well, it doesn't matter now. What I need is the will. Once it's destroyed, everything will be okay. Surprisingly, no one has seen it since the night of the party, but you know where it is. She signed it, didn't she... and you were her witness. You hid it for her. It's the only thing that makes sense. Where did you put it?"

"I don't have it."

"Don't lie to me, Vanessa. I've killed twice to get my hands on it. Another murder isn't going to make any difference. Give me the will."

"The police have it."

"The police? You little... That's a problem." She paced back and forth. Vanessa's eyes darted around the room. If only she could get to the door or even out onto the balcony. Her bare feet slipped sideways on the rug, inching toward escape. Adele stopped, piercing her in place with a laser pointed stare. Her eyes glazed as madness turned her countenance to a caricature of itself. "You should have told me about the will. I would not have had to kill Thomas, if I had known you'd seen

195

it last. He was telling the truth. He didn't have it. Oh well, couldn't take a chance. Because of you, my plans are in ruins. I'll need to get out of town for a while. A nice spa in the south of France. That would be lovely this time of year. Heaven knows, I deserve it. This whole ordeal has been terribly stressful. I need a diversion. Another death ought to do it."

"Another death?"

"Yes, dear girl. You are going to pay for what you've done. It will also keep the authorities busy and away from me. They'll blame Andrew as he has the most to lose. Such a pompous ass." Her pupils dilated as she moved in her soft sneakers toward her.

Vanessa's bright eyes opened wide in shock. "No, no."

"Oh, but yes, yes. I'm sorry, Vanessa. I like you. You've given Percy and me a lot of comic relief over the years and I do regret this, but you must be punished, and I need time to get away."

A sadistic grin split her face as she reached for Vanessa's throat, wrapping her hands around its soft whiteness, and squeezing. The door to the bedroom crashed open.

"Vanessa!"

Andrew flew across the room and slammed into Adele, which sent her crashing into the fireplace. She loosened her grip and Vanessa slumped to the floor. Adele shook her head and stared at her brother-in-law. "Ah, Andrew. The white knight come to rescue his damsel." A maniacal laugh erupted from her mouth. "It doesn't matter. The will has been signed and it's all gone. All my lovely money. Your stupid wife knew all along. Did you know that?"

"Shut up. I'm taking you to the police."

"Oh, no. I don't think so. I couldn't abide being in a cell. It would be the death of me," Adele tittered.

The two adversaries circled each other. Andrew lunged at Adele, but she sidestepped him, and he went flying out onto the balcony. Adele followed. Fueled by adrenaline and madness, she launched herself at Andrew knocking him off balance. A little flash of silver rushed at her, growling and barking. Latching onto Adele's ankle, Zeus bit as hard as he could.

"Get that mutt off me."

Adele kicked out her leg while the little dog kept a tight hold onto her ankle. Hopping around the balcony, Adele didn't see the wet leaves on the portico. Her feet went out from under her. Letting go of his prey, Zeus ran to Vanessa and licked her face over and over.

Arms whirling over her head, Adele tried to regain her balance, but gravity and a low balustrade worked against her. The last thing she saw as she fell through space was the look of shock and revulsion on Andrew's face. She screamed and felt her body split wide open as it was impaled on the ornamental wrought iron fence surrounding the garden.

Chapter Forty-Eight

ndrew picked himself up from the floor of the terrace and rushed to the stone railing. He stared in horror at the body of his sister-in-law. Vanessa ran to his side.

"No. Don't look. Come inside. We must call the police."

Andrew put his arm around his wife and led her back into the bedroom.

"She was going to kill me, Andy. She told me she was the one who ran me down last week and it was only because of a pothole in the road that she missed. She killed your mother and Thomas Winslow as well. All because of money. She hated Martha. I've never seen so much hatred in one person. She went mad with it. Oh, poor Percy. What's he going to do?"

"Shhh, Pet. I'm going to give you the medicine the doctor prescribed. I want you to rest and then I'll call the police."

Andrew went into the bathroom and retrieved a glass of water and a sedative prescribed for Vanessa. He came back into the room, helped her undress, and gave her the pill. She swallowed it and lay down. Andrew pulled up the covers and sat on the bed taking her hand in his.

"You're good to me, Andy Panda."

"I love you, my sweet. You have a rest now and when you wake up, we'll talk about Mother's plans for this place. She was right. A healing sanctuary for lost and hurt animals is beginning to sound particularly good. There's been too much death and destruction due to greed. I want to see what we can do to bring life and healing to the homestead. And she was right about Jared. If he'll let me, I'd like to help him run the place."

Vanessa closed her eyes, smiled, and murmured, "I'm glad. You're a good man, Andy Panda. Would you put Zeus up on the bed with me? We can keep him, right?"

Andrew bent down and picked up the little dog. Placing him on the bed close to Vanessa, he said, "Of course we can keep him. He's a hero. He may be little, but he certainly lives up to his name."

As Vanessa snuggled up with Zeus and drifted off to sleep, Andrew rose and went down to the living room. He stood behind his mother's desk staring out at the garden. Two deaths and he'd almost lost Vanessa. He thought of Martha.

"I miss you, Mother. What I wouldn't give to have you with me now."

Surprisingly, since she had died, he found himself missing her. It was not a feeling he had ever expected. Wandering around the property, he'd spent time talking to the hands and getting a clearer picture of what his mother wanted to do. He'd even had a pleasant meeting with Jared and Charli and listened to their hopes and plans. As the days wore on, he began to see the value of what they were talking about. Now he had seen the horror the love of money and greed produced, he questioned his own attitude toward them. How much did one person need anyway? Why did he need more and more? Wouldn't it be better to use what he had to help others? He didn't have all the answers, but he was on his way.

Martha and Gladys entered the room as Andrew spoke about missing his mother.

"Did you hear that, Gladys?" asked Martha.

"I'm standing right here, so I could hardly miss it." Gladys snorted.

"My boy misses me." Martha walked over to her son. Concentrating all her energy, she raised her hand and caressed his face. Andrew felt a touch like a feather stroking his cheek. "Mom," he whispered as a tear slid down his face.

Chapter Forty-Nine

S haking off his melancholy, Andrew reached for his phone. He was about to dial when he heard pounding on the front door.

"Police. Open up."

Andrew rushed to door and opened it to find Mac and Dr. Walsh on the doorstep. He escorted them into the living room.

"We heard a scream. What's going on?"

"I'm afraid there has been an accident. Mrs. Adele Bancroft has fallen from the balcony. She's dead."

"Where's the body?"

"It's around the back."

"Which balcony?"

"The one outside our bedroom."

"What happened?"

As Andrew related the bizarre events of the morning, Cissy called for her team. She left the room to find the body. As Andrew was finishing his tale, she re-entered the room and nodded to Mac.

"You say it was Mrs. Adele Bancroft who poisoned the toddy and she admitted to killing Thomas Winslow."

"Yes. She also tried to murder my wife but thank God for that pothole. Adele said she hit a tree, so maybe one of the cars has front-end damage. You can check on anything you like. The cars are in the garage."

"Thank you, Mr. Bancroft. We've already inspected the car. May I speak to your wife, please?"

"I have given her a sedative, Detective. She will be sleeping for a while. I'd be happy to have you talk to her when she wakes up. What a mess. How am I going to tell Percy? What am I going to tell him? He and his mother were close. This will devastate him."

"He does have his family around."

"Ha. He hates the lot of us… with good reason. None of us were particularly kind to either of them. We've got a lot of fence mending to do."

The group rose and walked out to where the accident had taken place. The paramedics had removed Adele's body from the spike and placed it on a gurney. Mac looked at her face. A paramedic had closed the eyes. Gone was the bitterness and malice. She again looked as he had first seen her; a cherubic maiden aunt who wouldn't say shit if she had a mouth full of it. He shook his head. How was the family going to heal? What would happen to the place now? Spring would be here in a few short months. Hopefully, it would bring new life to the Bancroft estate.

Chapter Fifty

Martha watched the surprise look on Adele's face as she approached her.

"Martha?"

"Hello, Adele."

"You're dead. I killed you. Why are you here? Where are we?"

"Surprise. Seems you fell off the balcony. You're dead too."

"Dead? But there's nothing when you die. It's over."

"Bit of a shock then."

"No, this can't be happening. I'm hallucinating."

"It's real."

Adele looked around her. She noticed Gladys and two shadow Beings nearby.

"Who are these things with you? Are they ghosts?"

"No, they are not ghosts. They're Herdsmen, angels, helpers, spirit guides…whatever you want to call them. Gladys is mine. The other two are for you, I guess. They're here to help your transition."

"Transition? To what? Where? I don't understand."

"To wherever you have chosen to go."

"What's that bright light? I feel like liquid fire is burning through every part of me. Get it to stop!"

Gladys moved closer to her. "The light is Love. It's where we belong. It's home. But you've been broken by the choices you've made. That's why it hurts. You can no longer tolerate it. Another place is ready for you where your energy will resonate. There will be others with you who vibrate at your frequency. Eventually, if you choose, and with the help of your Guides, you'll be able to heal, raise your vibration and tolerate the light."

"Keep away, you creep. There's nothing wrong with me. I'm fine. You can't do this to me."

"No one's doing anything to you. Go with your helpers, Adele. They will stay with you."

The Herdsmen encircled Adele and lifted her screaming away from the scene and out of sight.

"Take your hands off me. I'm not going anywhere. I'm Adele Bancroft! Do you hear me? I'm important in this town. That was my money. I deserved it. Let me go."

"Where's she gone, Gladys?"

"To a waiting place. Would you like to see it?"

"Can we?"

"Yes, but we can't stay too long. You haven't been home yet. You still resonate with earth's frequency. The energy in this realm will negatively affect you. Let's go."

A thick, gray fog swirled around swallowing them in its icy tentacles. Martha could hear cries and screams and her energy field dimmed. When the fog dissipated, a city landscape appeared in the distance. Desolation flooded her senses. Loneliness pierced her being like a sharp icicle sending pain throughout her energy field. The city felt like a cold, dreary late November day. There was no warm sun or beautiful flowers. No birds singing. Only darkness and dull shades of gray. As she walked the streets, the beings she passed could not see either her or Gladys, lost as they were in their own misery. A Herdsman accompanied each soul, but they neither welcomed nor even seemed to be aware of them. The atmosphere, infused with great loss and emptiness, encompassed every creature.

"Where are we? This place is dreadful," Martha whispered.

"A way station. A portal to the lower realms. When a human dies unexpectedly, they can be very confused. When that soul is broken by what they've done while on earth, places like this help them adjust to being dead before moving to one of the lower realms."

"But what if you've done a horrible act?"

"There are realms which hardly vibrate at all, where the density of energy is so great, spirits who are splintered because of their evil actions while on earth, are taken there immediately. It is the only place they will resonate without shattering completely. But even there, Love resides. This Love connects everything in the universe. It's what holds it all together. Even those souls can be transmuted or changed by that Love."

"Can a soul really heal and get out of the lower realms? I thought Hell was for eternity?"

"While on earth, with limited knowledge, many people, can't or don't want to believe a soul can be restored and move on from the hell it created for itself. They prefer punishment to restoration. We understand so little while in human form, but Love understands. And, yes, a soul can be changed by Love. It doesn't matter how long it takes."

"There's Adele, up ahead. She's going into that coffee place. Let's catch up."

Martha and Gladys followed Adele into the shop. Martha swooned at the feelings of anger, hatred, addiction, lust, despair, jealousy, and pride which permeated the atmosphere. Gladys caught her and infused some of her own light into her energy field.

"Whoa. I thought it was just an ordinary store where you grab a cuppa."

"Actually, none of the buildings or props are real. I told you; everything is energy. This landscape is an illusion made for those who are still attached to earth. It helps ground them. What you're feeling are their emotions. Nothing's hidden in this realm. I can help protect you for a while, but we need to move on soon."

"Okay. I just want to talk to her once more."

Martha moved over to where Adele was sitting.

"Adele."

She looked up, shocked at seeing Martha.

"Martha, what are you doing here?"

"I've come to talk to you."

"Leave me alone. You did this to me. It's your fault I'm stuck in this hell hole. But I have friends. They all welcomed me when I came in.

Hey, guys, come and meet my dear mother-in-law." Adele waved a group of entities over to her table. They came and circled her, grinning malevolently at Martha. "Go on. Get outta here. I don't need you," Adele snarled at Martha, anger shooting white hot current from her essence. Martha recoiled as a wave of hatred, self-righteousness and rage hit her energy field.

"Martha, it's time to go," said Gladys gently.

"Yes, yes, of course," murmured Martha struggling to escape the tentacles of darkness clawing at her.

Gladys and Martha left the shop and the city and moved back through the fog to the estate. Gladys called for assistance and other beings of light surrounded them. They infused Martha with light energy until she was vibrating at her own level. She turned to Gladys.

"That was horrifying. The density of the power was incredible. It drained hope and lightness from me. If we had stayed much longer, I would have been sucked dry and would not have been able to get out."

"And yet, Love and Hope are there, ready for anyone who will accept them. It's time to go. Your business is finished here."

"I've caused so much anger and hatred."

"Adele didn't have to react the way she did. She chose darkness and her choice caused her to shatter. She still has a chance to mend the broken pieces, but it's her choice. Love will wait until she's ready."

Martha looked at her.

"Right. It's time to go, but I have one more thing to do before I move on."

"For Pete's sake, what now?" huffed Gladys.

"Wait here. I'll be right back." Martha disappeared and headed straight for her old bedroom. Zeus was snoring on the bed. He perked up and wagged his tail when the apparition manifested at his side. Martha leaned over and kissed him. "Such a good boy. Mommy has to go away for a while. I want you to stay with Vanessa. She'll take good care of you until we see each other again when you cross the rainbow bridge."

Zeus gave a final woof goodbye and lay back down knowing he would see her again. Martha zoomed back to Gladys. "I'm ready."

A tunnel of very bright light appeared in front of them. Martha gazed at the tunnel and her essence glowed brighter.

"I see Bobby. He's holding out his arms and smiling at me. 'Bobby! Wait. I'm coming!'"

Martha zipped through the tunnel and into Robert's arms.

"Sheesh! That's all it took?" muttered Gladys.

Gladys sped after Martha. The bright light dissipated from the room. All was quiet at the Double O Ranch.

This novel is a work of **Visionary Fiction.** Locations mentioned in the book may be real, but details have been altered to weave a better story.

Visionary Fiction: A Definition

Besides telling a good story, VF enlightens and encourages readers to expand their awareness of greater possibilities. It helps them see the world in a new light and recognize dimensions of reality they commonly ignore.

This story is by no means an authoritative essay on the afterlife, but the Author's imagination at work at what it could look like.

Thank you for reading my book. I hope you enjoyed it. If you did I would ask for a quick review. It doesn't have to be long. Just a "I enjoyed the book" would be great. Here's the link to leave a review. https://www.amazon.com/Murder-Mothers-Scugog-Township-Mystery-ebook/dp/B073MWG4GT

If you wish to read more about Martha and Gladys, they can be found in the next book in this series: The Haunting of Hawk's Ridge Hall. Here's the first chapter.

Chapter One

Hawk's Ridge Hall had seen better days. In the Roaring '20s the Grande Dame of Scugog Township was the place to be for opulent soirées and nefarious skullduggery. Alas, she now stood in genteel dishabille, abandoned in the pre-dawn mist of mid-September.

Her magnificent wrought iron gate squealed like an out of tune violin as the wind played on its rusty hinges. A hawk, perched on one of her crumbling stone pillars, was focussed on a tiny field mouse scurrying across the unkempt lawn trying to reach the safety of the house. A blast of wind rustled dried leaves across the warped front porch swooshing through a broken casement window screeching like a Banshee.

Inside the house, grimy water stains cascaded down the wall creating grotesque patterns on the faded but elegant wallpaper. Dust motes stirred by the air current floated up the rickety staircase leading to the second floor. In the master bedroom, twin orbs of light danced in a sunbeam peeking through the window as the sun rose. They elongated into the apparitions of two women in their early seventies.

Gladys, tall and slender, was dressed in a flowing caftan of blue and turquoise. She looked around the room, hands on hips and asked,

"Where the hell have you landed us now?"

"What?" said Martha, turning her head to look at the back side of her blue silk pantsuit. She looked up. "Oh. Well, not there, that's for sure."

"What are you looking for?" asked Gladys noting her friend's actions.

"Just checking to make sure I'm all in one piece. One time I materialized; my bottom half was backwards." She shivered. "You have no idea how that made me feel."

Satisfied everything was where it was supposed to be, she looked around the room, lines creasing her forehead. "Hmmm. This doesn't seem right."

"Ya think?"

"So, my GPS is a little off! Recalculating."

"What are we doing here anyway? You never did tell me what's

208

going on."

"I figured you wouldn't come if I did." Martha blew out a sigh. "Look, I come back every once in awhile just to check on things. I've been watching Cissy and Mac. They've grown apart. They belong together, like Bobby and me, so I'm here to nudge them along."

"Cissy and Mac. I might have guessed," sighed Gladys. "Well, it looks like we're off to a great start."

"I know. Can't believe I miscalculated. I wonder why we landed here?"

The two ghosts strolled around the old bedroom.

"Doesn't look like anyone's been here in years," said Gladys as she pointed to the windowsill. "Look at the dust... and are those mouse droppings?" She gave a shudder. "Disgusting."

"You afraid there might be a ghost?" laughed Martha, wiggling her eyebrows. "C'mon, let's explore downstairs". With a flash she was gone. Gladys followed as they set about inspecting the first floor. "What a beautiful old place," said Martha as she scanned the front living room. "Needs a little work but look at that crown molding. Wherever we are, this house must have been something in its heyday. If only walls could talk."

"Maybe they'd have some idea why we're here." said Gladys with a smirk.

"Just 'cause I got a little off course; you don't have to be snarky. Let's go outside and see if we can figure out where we are." Changing into orbs to blend with the rising sun, they landed in the front yard.

"Doesn't look familiar to me. You?" asked Gladys.

"Nope."

"Now what?"

"I say we hang around for awhile and see what's going on. We must have landed here for a reason, but darned if I know what it is."

"It's not like I have anything else to do," sniffed Gladys. "I could be visiting another planet, or discussing philosophy with our group, but no,

I had to come with you."

Martha groaned. "Oh, for… you give me a headache. Let's settle in the bushes by the front gate. Something is going to happen. I can feel it in my bones."

"What bones? You don't have any."

"Ha ha. Very funny. Just be on the lookout. This, whatever this is, may be more than I bargained for."

"It always is," sighed Gladys.

https://www.amazon.com/Haunting-Hawks-Ridge-Scugog-Mystery-ebook/dp/B07QSBQRCN

Other books by the Author:

Novels:

> *Stone Cottage*
>
> *Murder at Mother's*
>
> *The Haunting of Hawk's Ridge Hall*
>
> *Finding Charli*
>
> *Witchfyre and Faerysong*

Anthologies:

> *Glimmers*

Children's stories:

> *The Mysterious Door*
>
> *The Hammer and the Sword*